LAKE CRESCENT AND OTHER SPIRITS

LAKE CRESCENT

ISBN 978-0-913123-52-2

Library of Congress Control Number: 2025942410

First published by Galileo Press in 2025
Aiken, South Carolina
online at www.freegalileo.com

Book design by Adam Robinson
Cover drawing by Pamela Gullard

AND **OTHER SPIRITS**

I want to lie with you and love with you
where suns rise and moons rise on the
purple edge outside most people's lives.

—EDNA ST. VINCENT MILLAY

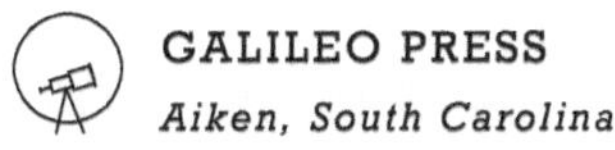

GALILEO PRESS
Aiken, South Carolina

CONTENTS

Love Came Suddenly to Me ...
1

Where is Ojai?
15

One Small Death Before the Plague
29

Atlantis
43

Slide it Closer to the Center
65

Wild Oats
79

A Man Like My Father
101

Listen
131

Hawk Wind
151

A Place for Fine Hats
175

Lake Crescent
199

Acknowledgments
217

For Mike

LOVE CAME SUDDENLY TO ME...

like the click before the release of a lock. I was twenty-nine and hadn't believed in letting go. Look around you. Who ever let go and didn't get hit? But there I was in love with Frederick, feeling, some nights, like a six-gill shark. Like I'd swim across the Sound just to touch his ankle, his shin, to lick his knee. A kiss. Higher. A taste. Another.

I'd known him for two moons. After one night livened by Andromeda being so fucking close to Earth, I woke early in his house, wandered in bare feet out to his deck and stood at the rail. Sun burst through the mist and lit up distant ice fields on Mount Rainier. The mountain rose before my eyes. I remembered Frederick's hand on my belly. He came to the door. The light caught against his heavy cheek and thick, blond brow. Deep cuts bracketed his mouth, showing his late nights working at the hospital. He said solemnly, "Is it too early to ask you to marry me?"

The light scattered. "No! Yes!" I was laughing. "Any time before noon is okay. Just let me find some underwear."

He took me in his arms with his big, slow smile. "I can't believe you swam all the way across last night."

A kiss. A taste.

I CALLED MY BROTHER, Stephen, that afternoon and told him I wanted to take him fishing. I would tell him at the river where Dad had taken us when we were young. In those days Dad would sometimes go to Virginia Mason at dawn to check on a dying patient, and then he'd take us to the river and nap on his back on the grass, and we'd wake him when the plastic bobber of his fish line went under. I was five and Stephen was seven. We felt the secret of the dangerous, rushing water and knew instinctively not to tell Mom.

I stood, shivering, at 6:30 a.m. on the narrow breezeway of Stephen's second-story apartment and knocked again. He'd set the early time. Behind me cars raced over the Okanogan highway for the hour commute to Seattle. I rattled the door. Stephen was probably still sleeping. I didn't want to be mad at him before the sun broke through, if it ever did. I listened for any stirring behind his door, wanting to dust my joy all over his shaggy, sleepy face.

Stephen was a sculptor. His giant nests of driftwood and men out of hay bales quickly aged in the Seattle rain. He got commissions from Microsoft or Boeing people who wanted to prove their art bonas without any long-term commitment to granite or marble. Stephen hated to hear how his work was wonderfully accessible, how it spoke about ephemerality. Like duh, he said. He teased me for my optimism, but I was the one he called when he couldn't find his car or his shoes.

He opened the door and pushed at the screen so I could step in. No shirt. Tied running pants. Dark hair smashed to one side, but the smell merely of stale sheets and the licorice gum he chewed obsessively when he was drawing, not the sweet alarm of gin sweat or the sick, sour ringing of burgundy or the sweat of vodka that's like mustard gas you've only heard about but that's seeped into your subconscious like your own hidden brutality.

"Hi," I said. "Now, if I were an alarm clock where would I be?" I pretended to Sherlock the room, holding an invisible magnifying glass up to my face.

I didn't see his girlfriend. Was Darius up early to go to work? I didn't know her well, but liked her—she was a steadying influence on Stephen. All about three squares and bedtimes and regular flossing.

He hugged me and stood there. "I thought I hit snooze," he said, "but I must have turned it off."

"Darius not here?" I asked.

He moved a stack of books off the couch and sat down. "Not here."

"C'mon," I said. "Get your jacket!" I could hardly ever rush my brother, but this morning was big enough to try.

He ran three fingers down the stubble at his jaw. "I was thinking… Whenever you ask me to go to the river—I mean, you know we can't go back."

I was hurt. "This isn't about the past." It was. I wanted to go back to the time before he or I knew much of anything. I thought of the morning we caught five fish before Dad woke up, and we didn't tell him or anyone. The fish flipped through the grass, and we kept ourselves silent, our mouths open with shouts as we danced around the slithering, panicked creatures. We caught them one by one. They were almost too slippery to hold, but we slid them into the water and watched them glide away, their wild gasps for life instantly transformed into a command of the water.

Today I wanted that Stephen. We had stood together and watched in awe as the fish took their paths into the darkness. I wanted to stop worrying about Stephen today. Let him go. Leave him behind. Love him again.

We got in my new Celica. I had a good job as admin to a group of five architects in Seattle. The architects were young and going places, and I liked the long silences that often rose from their work spaces as they concentrated. Stephen thought that liking my job was suspiciously close to selling out. Sometimes I wondered if I was the deeper cynic, but I didn't play that role. Stephen had never forgiven Dad when we realized he had other women.

I drove north on the highway for about a half mile, then into the farm country of rolling hills and apple orchards.

Frederick hardly moved when he slept. Long, slow breaths. Asleep, he was Fletch, my secret name. Silly. My arrow. Gripping my heart. I unwound my leg from his and kissed his closed eyelids. Nothing. "I'm going fishing," I whispered, my hand on his chest. The slightest quickening under my palm. "Don't leave." Instant consciousness, then the sinking back.

"The fish won't catch themselves."

Another rise to the surface. "They will."

"Save my place."

"I'm a vegetarian."

I gently bit his lip. "I'm a butcher."

We turned onto the gravel road that would drop down to the river. A small truck behind us slowed too. Had he been following us? The driver was small and wore a blue baseball cap. What was the matter with me? I had a day off. I was in love. My emotions were slipping around, but they didn't need to go into a sense of danger. Besides, no self-respecting axe murderer would be a Mariners fan, not with their pitching rotation.

I sped up, wet gravel flying. The Skagit River came into view, a placid swell of water past a stand of elms. Behind us the truck stopped and turned around. See. Nerves. My ordinary dark ghost. My brother dozed with his head against the window.

His latest big project had been a giant, kneeling man on Magnolia Bluff. He called me at 2 a.m. to say he'd finished and it was too dark to take the path so he was thinking of jumping off the cliff.

"I have a flashlight," I said, my heart pounding. I raced around my apartment pulling the folded blanket off my bed, pouring coffee into a thermos, finding my keys. Who'd taken my keys? There, in the bowl.

"I'm freezing," my brother said. "Elliott Bay will be warm." Glacial, actually. He'd quit trying.

"Take a picture. Stephen, right now. Take a picture toward the light. Sit down and send it to me." I held the phone with my shoulder while I clambered into the car. I pictured the boulders in the blackness thirty feet below the bluff.

"My phone doesn't work." He wasn't drunk. Worse.

"Don't give up."

"It's just a phone." His voice fading.

"You."

"Too late." Not much more than a whisper.

"Give me twenty-five minutes." No traffic. Maybe twenty. Westlake would be fastest from my place near Lake Union. I turned onto it.

Hardly a car on the road but cops hid near the pubs. Slow, slow. Five full minutes passed. My phone on the passenger's seat pinged with a message. My brother's photo.

"Okay," I said aloud. The glow of Seattle was to the southwest. He was at the spot where he and his friends in high school smoked weed. I said, "Now turn around and use the flash on your work."

"You know I don't use a flash." Good. Sarcasm. A spark.

"It's night," I said.

"Do you realize you're not making sense?"

"That's rich." Silence. "I'm waiting."

"For the night to pass?" Another dark bit. Good.

"For you to use the flash. Because it's night."

"Oh ya. Forgot my assigned task."

There was some traffic near downtown, then there wasn't and I went to seventy. I parked in someone's driveway and tore up the hill. Tree branches caught my jacket. There was mud. I slid back and hit my back against a trunk. Nothing seemed familiar. The trees had arrived in the night.

There he was, sitting on a leftover bale. We didn't speak. I threw the blanket around his shoulders and held him and held him. The kneeling man loomed. Darkness behind.

"I'm sorry," he said finally.

"I know."

"I just couldn't ... I just ... There wasn't anything left."

I said firmly, "We have to go now. You're shivering."

I heard the ocean below, as if someone had turned off the mute. He said, "You go. I need my zen moment with Mister." He looked up at the big square face of the sculpture.

"No zen moments. Time to go home." I pulled at his hand to stand him up.

He pulled back. "Not yours to say."

I could feel him sliding away from me again. "You stay. I stay."

He shrugged.

I would wait him out. Silence was my only weapon. I sat next to him. A half hour passed. I picked up a twig to fiddle with. Another. My shoulders were cold. My ankle was bleeding. I breathed slowly, six in, seven out.

He didn't move. He was gone to the world. I handed him the twig. He took it. Another. The moon was absent.

He said, "I can't make it work."

"Says the man sitting next to Colossus." I held up my phone and showed him the photo.

He looked a little startled, as if he'd never seen that large man. Then he wilted again. "It looks better than it is. My work is photogenic. Presto, bingo. I'm a major artist!"

"I didn't say you were a *major* artist."

He turned slowly toward me. The phone's light brought him out of the dark. He gave the slightest smile. I didn't move. My brother. My brother. A cloud balanced on a slight brightening that could have been the moon. Finally, he said, "You drive." We would find his car the next day. We knew how to do that.

IN A HALF MILE I pulled off the road and stopped near the table rock where Dad had often laid out our picnics. We got out and unloaded the bologna sandwiches with extra mayo that I'd made for lunch, our poles, and my tackle box. Stephen had lost his tackle years ago. We walked to the river, finding places in the hummocks of crabgrass that weren't too squishy for our sandals. This was a good place for fishing, an eddy with boulders on the bank to sit on.

I unlatched the box. The worms were in a tangle in a plastic hummus carton with holes I'd punched on top. No flies with pink feathers or manufactured bait. "Here," I said to my brother, holding out a new hook and a worm.

He shook his head. Dad had never been able to get him to thread the worm either. "You're a big boy now," I said.

"I still don't have anything against a worm."

"Then you can't hold your own pole." I smiled.

He nodded, amused. "I'll torture all the worms you want in the afterlife."

"How weird is that?" I pushed the point through the worm's alimentary canal, careful to avoid the tough collar. If we caught anything, I'd be the one to clean it. I was almost as good as Dad at slitting the belly from vent to craw and lifting out the intestines in one good finger scoop. Stephen told me that I'd learned a lot from Dad and that he'd learned nothing. I wasn't sure how to take that. Once, Dad had taken us to a big house on Capitol Hill for a house call. He disappeared for a long time in a back room with a woman who didn't look sick.

My brother said, "You're happy today."

I looked up. He was standing between me and the river. The breeze skittered dark hair across his forehead. He was only thirty-one but his forehead had deep lines from all his days outdoors wiring hay bales or walking the beaches finding wood. Stephen's early sculptures looked like stick huts. At the reception for his first show outside the Burke Museum on the UW campus, he told the little crowd that he owed his success to me, his chief gatherer. He was nineteen and made his first sale that day.

"I'm in love," I said quietly, "and you have to be nice about it." He usually had something to say about my boyfriends. *Did you notice that he's flat-out missing a sense of humor? That his sleeve tat is too dense—and that blue! Or is it azure?*

He took the pole and a couple of weights that were like split balls of shot. There was a beat as he pressed a weight around the line. Finally he said mildly, "Who's the lucky guy?"

"You're supposed to jump up and give me a hug."

"But you sound like someone died." He didn't move.

"Frederick."

I slid on the next worm, my fingers sticky with its scum.

"Frederick," Stephen said. He cast the line in the water and quickly wedged the pole against the rock. "Sounds nice."

"Why are you being like this!"

"For God's sake, Lise, you haven't told me anything yet. I know his name. Frederick the Great. How can I be happy for you?"

I cried, "See. See! You just had to say that!" I savagely cast my line and it almost crossed his.

"Lise, stop. I get it. You want me to like this guy. I like him, okay? And someday I'll actually know something about him."

"He's a pediatrician. He rides a bike to work." Frederick the Great. I'd never get that out of my head. Sometimes Frederick gave that little squint when he answered a question. A flick of arrogance, nothing more.

"A doctor," Stephen said.

"Yes." The breeze bowed both our lines sideways over dark water.

"Like Dad."

"He's nothing like Dad."

There was just the lapping of the water. "I *am* happy for you," Stephen said sorrowfully.

We were sitting side by side on the rock. "You've got Darius," I said. I didn't want to talk about Darius. I patted his back.

He nodded. "She's a good person."

That old subject, which we usually covered when he was drunk. Whenever he was with a woman, he was 100% loyal, he said. His slips meant nothing, they just happened, he wasn't sure why. If I agreed or didn't, he'd end up shouting at me. His main slip was the curator at the Burke and his so-called agent. She had long, curly, white hair and was twenty years older than he was. He often went to her when he was about to end things with someone else.

I said, "And you're a good person." The breeze picked up; we'd have to reset our lines soon. "Can be," I added.

He nudged my shoulder and ducked his head. Compliment accepted. My spirits rose. Okay.

We barely talked for an hour. We cast farther out but didn't catch anything. The cool morning brought a freshness to the river that I'd almost forgotten. Darius worked at Nordstrom in the fine jewelry department. She had a tat of roses at her collarbone and used her employee discount to upgrade the diamond in her nose. Stephen and I had waited for her at work a couple of times. She could handle the bougies, the ultra cool, and my brother.

A lost Canada goose landed one hundred yards out and rode the waves, bobbing up and down. Everything was going to turn out fine. In the next few minutes I'd tell Stephen that I was getting married.

A month ago I was driving in the U. District and saw the curator on the sidewalk. That flying white hair was hard to miss. She was with someone I couldn't quite see. I turned the corner so I wouldn't know. My mind tightened. *Was* I marrying my father? Frederick was so different from Dad. Most mornings Dad worked with a hangover. Frederick only drank hard after twelve-hour days—who could blame him? My brother had tried to cast doubt but I wouldn't take it. There was no dimming. None.

A tug at my bobber. I gave a good jerk to set the hook. The bobber travelled in a circle. Stephen said, "All right! All right." I was the one who usually caught something, and he was always a good audience.

I held the line tight and began a steady reel back. The fish tried to head into the current. I held it. Another circle. I pulled up and the mid-sized perch was mine. I didn't even need to put the net in the water. I dumped the fish in the cooler.

"One down," Stephen said, smiling at me.

I re-baited the hook and we settled down again. I tried not to think. Dad, a heart specialist, was sarcastic about the "worried well" with nothing better to do than count their heartbeats. Frederick worried about "his" kids and their parents, even the ones who got intense about a cold. Except for the science of his work, Dad was careless to the core. Once, Mom left for her sister's, and he forgot to pick up Stephen from soccer camp. Stephen waited in a parking lot for five hours.

I looked at him. He had his hood pulled up over his head, his forearms on his thighs.

I wanted to leave while we had our nice peace. I said, "You look frozen. Maybe we should go. I'm glad for this..."

I turned to a noise. Darius running toward us, her short skirt flying, her baseball cap jammed onto her head, her hightops caked with mud. The guy in the truck. She was screaming at Stephen. "I tried to just go home and pack. I tried! You fucker! Who was it? Tell me who it was! I just have to know that. Then I can go."

He stood up just as she swung at him, knocking him a step back against the boulder as he held up his open palms.

"What?" he said.

"Antibiotics will cure it!" she screamed, her face close to

his. "Just so you know. A small thing, Stephen. Nothing to worry about. No permanent damage. To you. To me. Like I didn't even know you. Thank God!" She gave his chest another shove.

"What? Tell me what you're talking about. We can talk about this."

"Don't even say it."

She turned to me. "I just wanted you to know who your brother is. That's it. Spread the pain." She looked at me. "Oh, I see, you already know. Fuck. I can't even find someone to knife."

I was stung. Tainted. The morning tainted. "Go away," I said to her.

She looked around as if seeing the river for the first time. "Well, yes. My work here is done," she said sarcastically and walked away.

Stephen didn't move. The river was a rush in my ears. I had the strong sense that he had to speak first, take this on his own. I sat down, my pole in my hand. His pole was still wedged in the rock, his line drifting to the shallows. I left it that way. Mine had caught a current and moved farther out. Stephen sat down beside me.

Minutes passed. His sorrow filled the breeze. I didn't want his sorrow. Whitecaps rose on the river. The fish would drop down to the sandbar. He said, "I can't lose her."

"You loved her," I said savagely, to make him feel worse.

He turned to me. "Okay, I get it."

"What do you get? You don't get anything."

"It was a mistake!"

"A mistake? You're a jerk, *just like Dad*," I said.

He turned. "What are you doing? Why are you being like this? She was the one. I don't know what I'm going to do."

"Poor Stephen."

He put his hand on my shoulder. "I see. You too."

I didn't look at him.

He dropped his hand, turned, his head down.

I would not go to him.

I sat apart. There was another fish. He hadn't gotten the message to hide deeper. I pulled it in. Stephen didn't move. I fished.

Stephen sat turned away on the rock. The breeze became wind. We were sitting in a near gale. My line bowed out above the waves.

Stephen said, "Maybe you'll have children someday."

"Yes. We're getting married and we'll have children. Old story. We'll try the old story. Suspend disbelief." I started to retrieve my line, a fast clicking.

He turned a little and nudged my shoulder. "You'll teach them what you know." He offered peace now? Too late.

"I'll do that," I said. The waves blurred with my confusion. He leaned his back against mine like a chair, the way we'd sat while Dad slept. I could feel his shoulder bones and the hard muscles from lifting bales and hoping to make something he could live with.

"Good," he said finally, as if answering a question. "Children should have a mother who knows how to gut a fish."

I stopped the reel. I couldn't see anything. There was the warmth of my brother's back. We didn't move. The two of us on a rock. Just that. Just that. Then, slowly, the river reappeared.

OUR BARE FEET UP on the rail of Frederick's deck, a box of Triscuits between us. The sound of gulls stuffed from scraps left by last beach picnics. I held up a cracker. "I'm glad you don't have elevated tastes."

He looked at me with a smile. "I do."

We were at the edge of the day between sun and enough darkness to see the moon. I often talked about my brother, and he asked about my visit.

"Good," I said. "He's in a good place." Mostly. "Working."

He nodded, not quite buying it. At the clinic, he often sorted through incomplete stories.

I took his hand on the table between us. "Can I call you Fletch?"

"Nope."

We laughed.

"I want him to be my best man."

No hesitation. "To codify the truth."

The wind had died. The cooling of the earth. "Yes."

The long, still pause as land and sea struck a truce. A child came tearing across the beach below, reached down and picked up a rag. No, a towel, and ran back to the trail.

"I need to meet this guy."

WHERE IS OJAI?

"He was a mistake, I was a kid." Alyssa said.

David touched her shoulder. "Go to the celebration," he said. "Say goodbye to him."

"Done and out. No goodbye necessary."

"Your mistake," he said.

"Harsh."

A Lyft driver swung around David's car and parked right next to a family yanking luggage up the curb.

"I want to see the house," she said. She and Jimmy had lived there for two years. "Say goodbye to *it*. Take the money and run."

Jimmy had bequeathed her the house. No explanation.

The plane reached cruising altitude over San Francisco. She brought up the street view of her old neighborhood in Ojai and zeroed in on the low, pink bungalow. She turned the avatar to the house. No one had repainted the green window frames. Was that a shadow in the kitchen? She'd taught Jimmy how to roll out pastry dough right there where the shadow was standing.

Jimmy Acheson. She'd married him when she was twenty-three; he was two years younger. They were free spirits. She loved Ojai's delicate air, as if a great cloud of *maybe* hung over the town. She loved Jimmy's contempt for the future. She dropped out of law school at UCLA, made berry pies from her mother's recipe, and sold the pies to local restaurants. He had enough family money to get by, painted houses when he felt like it, and spent most of his time in the hills smoking up with his rich friends.

Into her mind came a long, lazy Saturday afternoon in the house, her weekend pie deliveries done. She'd rubbed flour on the cutting board and placed the ball of dough on it. "You have to understand that for crust, perfect equals not good."

"Alyssa speaks," Jimmy had said. He stood behind her and leaned over her shoulder to watch.

"Now don't distract me." Her hands were covered in flour. "Don't work it too much, it will get tough." She wanted to teach him something; show him she had something to teach.

He rested his forearms on her breasts. "Don't work it," he repeated solemnly.

"Ha," she said, but she didn't want sex. Those days were filled with desire; he was hardly her first, but he kindled a heat that later bloomed with other men, other times, and then to David, but started with him.

That heat came over her on the plane. Turned on by a dead man. Her body rose, damn it, and her face burned, though no one could see. Even now she didn't want to give in to him. He'd never understood how valuable she was. No matter what he stole from her, he acted like it was nothing much. She opened the tray table, and it dropped with a crack. She had a novel by Sebastian Barry. A land laid waste. The bloody ache of civil war. She put the book in the pocket netting.

She caught the strap of her carry-on with her toe and took out the creased letter from Jimmy's lawyer. David had gone into the recycling and salvaged it, saying she might need it for legal purposes. He was a careful guy, but today, even that didn't seem right. Nothing was right.

Watson, Elliot, and Watson on the letterhead. *It has become our duty to inform you that James (Jimmy) Acheson died on April 10, 2016 of cardiac arrest.* Page two: a formal letter of instructions for accepting this gift. One of the Watsons had enclosed the obituary from the *L.A. Times*. Local boy makes good. Local boy steals wife's recipes and techniques, builds a multi-million-dollar company of frozen pies and tarts you can find in every good grocery store west of the Mississippi, beats his wife in court, and oh, by the way, breaks her stupid, naive heart, now healed. There would be a celebration of life at the Fair Winds Retreat in Ojai this coming Saturday, May 12 at 1 p.m.

He'd left her the house.

She would go to the celebration, and fly home. She would contact a real estate agent, and fly home. Get an assessment, put the property on the market, and fly home.

Case closed.

The walk-up line at Avis in the Bob Hope Airport was almost at a standstill. Someone had forgotten a license. Someone else needed a sedan. Alyssa calmed as she waited—she had lots of time. She and David had lived on the cool northern California coast for over twelve years; Ojai was just a twinge of regret from long ago. Her soft-spoken, apologetic mother had once told her that if you made happiness a goal, it would never come. People in line shuffled forward a few steps.

Alyssa liked her job as in-house lawyer for a company that ran refrigerated trucks out of Humboldt County across the west. And David brought surprises. A professor of philosophy at Humboldt State, he spent hours puzzling over thick texts, saying that he loved the struggle of getting close to life's knotted mysteries. But existence had to be more than a crossword puzzle where every clue was life and every answer was life that no one could solve. "Don't you want to do more than get *close*?" she'd asked him.

He'd nodded solemnly. "Walk into the flame, yes." He'd smiled. *"Coming?"* He began Jack Flash jumping around the room. In the mornings she'd sometimes wake with her upturned face against his ribs, his tortoise heartbeat on her cheek. Her mother was wrong.

SHE DROVE THE HONDA north through Ventura, over the low Topatopa Mountains, and into the bowl of Ojai. Mottled clouds turned a slight orange above the setting sun. She'd almost forgotten the Ojai air that carried the remembrance of the ocean forty miles away, the hard dirt of the Central Valley from the other direction, and its own lilies, leftover hippies, seeded bread those hippies still baked for tiny restaurants, and dusty blackberries that could be picked roadside and made into a pie.

The lawyer had said she could pick up the key from him, but instead she drove straight to the pink house behind the organic wine-tasting room and stopped.

The house seemed to have sunk through the years, the door to the side yard where she'd tried to grow figs listing to the side. Scraggly-caned roses gone to hips. Dirty windows. An aging cottage for a half-million dollars.

Jimmy had left her a puzzle she couldn't solve. At the divorce, she'd begged him to sell her his half. He'd refused and the chirpy real estate agent working for him had "liquidated" it for a pitiful sum of cash that she and Jimmy divided. Jimmy must have bought back that house when he prospered.

He missed her.

She walked over the tilted stepping stones and knocked, just to be sure there were no drifters, and there was Jimmy, as alive as could be, with deep ruts across his forehead, his boyish way of looking amused at whatever he saw, the dry stalks of blond hair raking across his brows. She stepped back. "You aren't…"

"Probably not." A slight shift of chapped lips that let the faint amusement cross his eyes. "But you are…?"

"Wrong house." She kept backing up. He was a ghost and she had a real ticket home in her suitcase. "I need to check some paperwork."

A worn smile. His eyes were bloodshot, his tan a blotch of freckles and red spots as if he'd been crying or roaring while pulling the wings off something, but wait, he was young, too young to be Jimmy, probably early twenties, but exhausted or possibly drunk.

She said, "I'm looking for Jimmy."

"Aren't we all." He glanced down. "The bastard." He squinted against an emotion she couldn't picture. "I'm his son." He looked up. "Let me guess. An ex-girlfriend." He looked at her. "Or ex-wife?"

"They come knocking every hour?"

"I'm having a wake."

The small living room had been turned into an office with shelves holding plastic boxes of manila files, an Ikea desk shoved under the low windows, two computers angled toward a straight-backed chair, a small, light table by the hall to the bathroom. "Graphics," he said. "I'm a graphics designer," and he nodded, as if that made him think of something else. By the couch was a round table that was bare except for a bottle of Chivas and a paper cup.

He lifted the desk chair so it faced the couch and said, "I'm Elijah, named for my father's brief religious phase. Welcome to my kingdom. Former kingdom. About to be tossed out, thank you very much, Dad. So much for finally getting started." He looked at her. Frowned. "I'll get you a glass."

Alyssa sat on the chair. He didn't realize yet that she was the wife in the will. The moment tightened. The juncture of walls and ceiling was sloped, and she remembered being gently cupped by the house, held by it, safe just before some nameless journey.

She'd been so young. Sweet maybe, she couldn't remember. She remembered Jimmy sitting on the couch, his hand on her thigh. Sadness shifted inside her like bags of sand being moved. She didn't know what to cry for.

Elijah returned and sat on the kitchen side with his long legs straight, like Jimmy's. A pleasant smell of garlic wafted from the kitchen.

"I was born in this house," he said.

"I lived here."

He looked at her. "Oh." A pause. "I see. It's you, all the way from Humboldt."

She nodded.

He downed half the cup, looked at it, turning it. "He gave it to me too."

"Not in the will."

He set the cup down. "No. The *will*, two sentences: 'I give everything to Miss Aging Cutie, my fourth wife. And the rest I give to First Wife X.'" He ran a hand down his T-shirt, Jimmy's gesture. "Not an exact quote."

His sorrow crept over her. Born here! His history layered on top of hers, smothering hers. "You could buy me out."

"What part of 'starting over' don't you understand?"

She stood, felt faint. "I can't do this." She gestured vaguely to the interior of the house, the small, dark hall that led to the bedroom and spare room. With alarm, she caught herself wanting to run down the hall and out the back door, see how the little garden was doing, revisit everything. "I wasn't expecting..." She turned back. "Everything's exactly the same! Except..." Where was her purse? In the car. Getting stolen. "I don't have to do this." Her mind gathered. She didn't. "I'm staying at the Chantico Inn," she said. "I want the keys in my hand by ten a.m. tomorrow. You can leave the heavy things and send for them later." Sometimes she had to ask company drivers for their keys. Asking worked. No one wanted cops and everyone wanted to save face. Drop the keys on my desk, she'd say. "Throw" was OK—she didn't mind the dents by her blotter.

"Bitch," Elijah said, defeated.

She didn't want to think about his defeats, his lost father. She fled.

THE SMALL HOTEL ROOM had an overstuffed chair crammed between front window and high bed so, for a moment, the bed seemed inaccessible. Her mind cleared and she went around. Fully clothed, she got under the covers. Some clock was ticking. She imagined the pillow smelled of the same detergent used by her mother. She tried to sleep, then did sleep.

She awoke at 9 p.m. with a picture of a sailboat in her mind. She sat up. This was the sailboat she'd buy for

David. He hated the cold, year-round fog of Bayside, but there weren't that many jobs for philosophy teachers and he liked his colleagues. Sunday mornings he and Alyssa would sit with their coffees at the marina, and he'd often say that one day he would win the lottery, and they'd buy a sailboat and sail it down after summer school to someplace warm. Now she could do that. She could finance David's dream. Imagine. Even if they just dumped the money in a retirement fund, *could* buy is 100 percent different from pure dream. Or she could buy a new car without thinking. Plane tickets to Montreal. She always wanted to walk the cobblestone streets of Old Montreal where even the French word for raspberry stayed on your tongue.

There was a knock at the door.

"I have plenty of towels," she called out. "Thanks!"

"I'm not the maid."

Elijah! Her thoughts made him exist! "Do you have the keys?"

A pause. "Yes."

She threw off the covers. One shoe was stuck at the bottom of the sheets. She took off the other one and padded to the door. He stood back on the little breezeway as she opened the door. Nothing in his hands.

She shut the door.

"Please," he said. "I just want to talk to you."

"There's nothing to say."

"I lied."

She waited. No footsteps. He wasn't leaving or explaining further. The quiet drivers who got caught were the hardest. They didn't try to explain why they couldn't make it to San Diego without getting high. They just hung their heads and asked for forgiveness. She'd tell them she wasn't in a position to forgive, and then she'd go home to cry.

She opened the door. People had to have their say before they could move on. "I was just going out," she said. "Maybe you can walk me someplace to eat."

"It's almost nine-thirty. This isn't New York City."

She glanced up. That faint smile. "And quit looking like him."

He ducked his head. "Doing my best."

It was a Mexican restaurant with a closed-off grocery section in the back. There were no other customers. Elijah had a Dos Equis, and she had a double enchilada that oozed a delicious, salty white cheese—cotija—she'd never had before. The server with a dishtowel pinned at the back may not have said a word, Alyssa couldn't recall. She was having trouble tracking the minutes. But she was ravenous and she ate. He took his time. She could wait out most people.

"I should have said I'm his *biological* son."

"All evidence to the contrary."

That smile.

"My mother took me to St. Louis when I was a baby. She didn't want to have anything to do with him." A pause. "He didn't fight it. Just let me go."

That sadness. She blocked it out. "OK."

He moved his cocktail napkin. "OK." He took one of her chips. "Last year I looked him up, and that house was one of the addresses that came up. I lived there for six months before he noticed." Another chip. "They should have brought salsa."

She pulled the plastic basket to her side of the table. "You weren't actually looking for him. Just a place to stay."

He shrugged. "I was looking for him," he said flatly. He

thought about that. "My shrink said I wanted *him* to find *me*." He signaled for another beer. She asked for the check. He could drink alone, finish the chips. She didn't need his story on top of hers.

He continued. "But no dice. I set up shop, placed an ad, walked downtown every day. Nothing. I guess he spent most of his time in L.A."

She was exhausted. "You had to get out of St. Louis," she guessed.

He took a breath. "Have you ever been to Missouri? I needed a state with a better attitude."

"And different law enforcement."

He looked at her sharply. "You're not like my mother." A pause. "What do you think I did?"

"Nothing much probably. Mostly involving weed or a DUI or two or both."

There was silence. She stood up but the waitress was nowhere to be found.

He said quickly, "OK. You're tough, I get that. Jimmy didn't give me the house."

"Hey there," she called out to the back of the restaurant. "We're leaving. There's some money on the table."

He got up with her, not leaving any money, his voice rising. "Jimmy said I could live there for a year! You could do that too. You get the equity. You saw the prices. Ojai is paradise. Ojai will always be paradise. Win/win."

"No," she said. When she was his age, she was married to his father. "Don't be a baby. He's not going to give you what he's not going to give. You can't force him. He can't see you. He's gone. He's always been gone. I'm talking crazy and I'm going to stop!" She looked at the table, then stared at him.

Finally he fished in his jeans and pulled out some bills that looked like ones.

She slapped a twenty on top. "You can understand—I don't want to be tangled up with Jimmy's ghost."

"I can't help what I look like. I hardly know him!" he cried. She turned away.

"Not fair," he said bitterly, following her into the fresh night. She tried to remember which way.

The street was black. "And I'll thank you to keep your grief to yourself," she said.

"I'm not grieving. Just..."

"Me too. I'll see you at eleven."

SHE WAITED UNTIL NOON. She called David. He asked how things were going, and she said OK, she was about to see the lawyer, get the sale started. She'd tell him about Elijah when they had more time.

At the Celebration of Life, chairs had been arranged in semicircle rows on the blindingly green grass of the lawn in front of an arc of old resort cabins turned into a spiritual retreat. Hand-painted vines and sunflowers crept up and around the small doors of the cabins. Some of the inhabitants sat on the little porches, placidly watching the crowd of mourners duck under the real bower of clematis and gather by the long refreshment table under a huge pepper tree. They held each other for long hugs.

Jimmy's widow had shiny gray hair. It fell in a short, straight waterfall as if it were poured.

She was tall, too thin, her stylish dress falling from bony shoulders, bare legs, red heels. She looked hollowed out but she greeted everyone.

Alyssa thought she smelled pastries. She sat in one of the white chairs as far away from the refreshment table as possible. No Elijah. She put her purse on the seat beside her. Despite everything, he should say goodbye. He only had one father. She felt drab in her gray suit. Almost all the other women wore flowered dresses. Ojai, land of flowers. Perfumed air sparkled off damp petals. Someone must have watered in the morning. She thought of the morning scent of the roses at the house, standing barefoot long ago, sated, on the front step. Young. Loved. Jimmy had stolen that girl on the step and moved on.

And so had she. She wanted to leave but knew she had to wait for Elijah. He had to come! She willed him to appear. People had apparently been told to sit, and they suddenly filled the chairs. A woman in a damask jacket looked at the purse, and finally Alyssa took it on her lap, and the woman took the chair. He could stand at the back. There was a violinist. A soprano belted out "Down to the River We Pray" into the fine, cardamom air. A minister in a bright-blue suit said some words.

Where was Elijah?

People got up and said that Jimmy was one of a kind, his own master, a comet, someone who made his corner of the world a brighter and crazier place. No one talked about loyalty and few mentioned friendship.

Alyssa rose, thinking wildly that if she spoke, Elijah would come. He had to say goodbye. That was the definition of a son, someone who said goodbye to his father, over and over, goodbye, goodbye.

She walked to the front, her heart pounding. She looked at all the people. They seemed like a field of flowers. She said, "I knew Jimmy a long time ago. He was very young then, and he didn't really see me." She glanced at the widow in the front, who didn't move. She was mourning but she was no fool.

Alyssa breathed the pure air. "But Jimmy, I see you. I see you charming the halos off the angels."

The audience laughed. "And then taking your cut."

They laughed harder.

Her heels were sinking into the grass. "I'll keep this short. But I want to tell you about Jimmy and the sun." She closed her eyes for a second. "One afternoon we climbed up to Manzanita Ridge to watch the sunset. He showed me how. He brought folding chairs and we set them in the weeds on rough ground. The chairs rocked when we moved. I wanted to look east to see the color reflected on the cliffs, but he told me that was for tourists. We were going to look west, like God intended."

There was a little laugh from the crowd. They could picture him saying that. She continued. "He showed me that if you hold your hand out with your arm fully extended and measure from the horizon, each finger counts for fifteen minutes before sunset." She held out her hand for a second. "We sat for almost an hour in silence, every so often measuring the sun's drop. Finally it sank right over the highway. He didn't move, just kept staring. It was getting dark. I asked him what he was doing. 'Holding the sun in my mind,' he said. 'I hold it just over the horizon. Don't let it drop. Everything stops. No death. You felt it, didn't you.'" Alyssa paused. Everyone was quiet. She said, "So if the sun doesn't go down today, you know who's behind that."

The widow laughed a little along with the others.

It was 2:00 on a Saturday afternoon and Jimmy was dead. She didn't tell the crowd that Jimmy had stood up in the sudden coolness and pulled her up and held her close, but she could tell he was thinking about something else. In that moment she knew, without a doubt, that he didn't love her. The coming night touched her back. It was a soft, fragile darkness that seemed unmoored from the falling sky. A magnolia loomed just to the side of her vision. She could feel its machinery of sap, respiration, its breath in the night.

With a start, she looked at the audience. She didn't speak, her mind flying, *Oh, Jimmy. Come back! I want to hate you again with all my heart.* She had kissed his neck, a soft, desperate kiss to hold off the next moment.

The audience waited and her shoulders eased. No reason. She had to finish what she was saying, nothing more, and so she spoke the old, calm word, "Godspeed." The crowd shifted in their seats as they felt her winding it up. "Godspeed, Jimmy." A few repeated it with her as the sun held the blinding grass.

More people came to the front and spoke, and then they all started to drift away.

Elijah slouched under the pepper tree. He didn't move so she went to him. "You can start painting the house tomorrow."

ONE SMALL DEATH BEFORE THE PLAGUE

Gerry was a ringer. He played for whatever tennis club on the peninsula would have him for the season. At age forty-one he was at the lower rung of the 40+ league, faster than the huffing guys a decade older and still hitting a good, heavy, deep ball from his days as number-one singles on his high school team in Milpitas. Muscles remembered, he sometimes thought with amazement, no matter how lonely or confused the rest of you got.

The lights on poles over the tennis courts at Junipero Club gathered cones of marine mist. Planes headed for SFO occasionally broke through the steady thunk of the balls, but the early September evening was pleasant, with pockets of cooler air from the bay traveling across still-warm courts. Gerry's opponent, a tall guy with a wide sweatband around his bald head, had a wicked slice and quick hands. Gerry won the toss and served first; he took the game but only after several deuces. This match was going to be harder than he'd expected.

At the changeover Gerry realized he'd forgotten his water bottle in the fridge. Damn. He poured water from the cooler into one of the club's dinky paper cups and gulped it. This would be a night of chasing thirst. His opponent—Bill? Bob?—said, "Sorry to hear about Luke."

"Yeah." Gerry hardly knew Luke, the guy he was playing for.

His opponent frowned as if that wasn't the right answer.

What happened to Luke? Usually it was some kind of ankle injury or a rotator cuff, not enough to mention. Gerry looked at his opponent.

"Dropping dead just when your last kid's graduated college. What a deal."

Dead?

"You never know." No longer on earth. Gerry's chest tightened.

The opponent sipped a cloudy, blue power drink. He had another two bottles of it lined up on his side of the bench, Nadal style. "He was in better shape than me," he said. "The heart's a funny thing. I heard that he'd just had a physical and passed with flying colors."

"Crying shame." Cool sweat sprang up on Gerry's face, the backs of his hands. A strange exhilaration rose through him, playing for a dead man. "Hard to know what to say."

"Yeah." The opponent headed to the service line and picked up the three balls at the T. He quickly called the score and served an ace.

Gerry hadn't been ready but let it go. Some guys snuck in a few quick-serves, and you looked like a whiner if you complained. Now he knew.

A woman was sitting under a tree on the viewers' mound in the spot by the third table, where Luke's wife usually sat. Had she been there all along? Luke's wife was often a quiet bystander who enjoyed the game but didn't play. Strange that she would come out alone so soon.

The opponent served another ace out wide that Gerry couldn't come near. His feet were suddenly lead. She must have been in the sleepwalk state, hardly knowing what she was doing. She tilted her head, a faint movement Gerry caught out of the corner of his eye. The tree rattled its dark leaves above her, backlit from the entry light in the clubhouse kept on 24/7 to discourage kids climbing the fence for a midnight swim.

In the past Gerry had barely noticed her, though once she'd handed him a beer after a match, and a light, peppery scent had lingered for a moment. It was so faint he hadn't been sure if it was from food or perfume, more a shift in the air around her. She wasn't what you would call good-looking but there was something. Lively, intelligent shifts of expression. The lift of her chin, her neck bare of jewelry.

The opponent's next serve toss was too low, and this time Gerry got a racket on it, but the ball shot off into the next court. 40-love before he'd blinked.

"Nice serve, Boyd," she called out from the little hill, her voice husky. Gerry looked directly at her, a small woman under a tree, her grief so new and baffling that she was cheering for the wrong side. Well, at least she'd given him a name: Boyd.

Gerry got set. A surge of strength coursed through him. He sent a vicious return up the line that made Boyd stumble back as he scrambled for it. Then Gerry struck an easy put-away. Ha. He glanced over at the widow in victory, ridiculously proud of himself, playing for her, the gladiator making her feel a little better.

But she called out to encourage Boyd, "Next time!" Wait. She was *trying* to cheer for the other guy.

Two more hard-fought points and Gerry lost. Total score 1-1. The woman clapped for Boyd.

Her husband must have died about two weeks ago, his name still on the last posting of the lineups. He was maybe fifty so they could have been married thirty years, then poof. Gerry stuffed a ball in his pocket, left the other one at the fence, and served out wide and high. Boyd couldn't come near it; it skittered off to the next court, and he quickly loped after it.

Beyond, the bay had blackened to empty space, no lights in the east where they should have been. Must have been a thicker fog over there. Gerry had been married for seven years, five years before the baby and then officially two more. Stillborn—not a baby. When the heartbeat went silent, the doctors induced. Gerry had cried for two days, and then it was over for him. They were young. They had lots of time; the doctors said there was no reason it would happen again, but Kristy couldn't get over it.

The next game seesawed for over ten minutes, the widow's voice floating into the night whenever Boyd lobbed high over Gerry's head or sliced the ball along the net so Gerry could only stand and watch. Sweating hard, his shirt soaked, he finally won and trotted over to her. He had to set this straight.

She looked up at him with just her eyes. Large, clear eyes. Lipstick. Hair with streaks of gray clipped back. But cheeks like something that had been peeled, white, the small lines contouring over stark bones. No confusion there. She'd been struck by lightning and knew it. He was the muddled one. "I'm sorry," he said, somehow not wanting to use that final phrase, "for your loss." An odd sense of failure came over him.

"Yes." Nothing more. She was deep in her own thoughts.

"You OK?" he asked. Idiot.

She didn't bother with sarcasm or any sound. Inside the club a few people leaving the club bar moved past the light, causing the darkness to waver back and forth.

"Sorry for that...I don't know..."

She nodded.

What now? He couldn't just turn around and go back to the court. The quickness in his chest felt like strings breaking.

Finally she moved her chin a little, as if slightly coming to life, and said, "Here's what you want to know. My sister just left. One daughter had to go back to La Jolla to work, and the other just got a job near my sister in Marin. My goddaughter is babysitting me until the weekend. I snuck out the window."

"You didn't." Even his admiration seemed babyish next to her monumental sadness.

She stared at the courts, five blue rectangles within chain-link fences, the farthest one slipping into blackness like an infinity pool.

He said, "I have to go play."

She nodded. "He's noticed that you don't step back enough for your overhead." She faintly lifted a brow. "Your ego makes you think you can get it."

A small cut, not a big one, but a little thud of dread rose through Gerry, as if he'd been attacked or was about to be attacked. He couldn't remember whose serve it was and just headed mid-court while Boyd finished toweling off at the side. The dread was a stone weighing him down, like the morning fear from a dream. He told himself that of course she would be all-powerful for a while, uncaring what mere mortals thought, cutting or kind, feeling no difference. With a start he remembered the feeling from a long time ago. The widow had walked off the cliff into thin air and anything could happen. Someone might save her or she could drop into a hole in the earth.

The mesh windscreens hanging from the chain-link fence looked flimsy, the painted court lines cartoonish. Suddenly daytime seemed far away, the sun rolling away with the expanding universe, leaving only a dark breeze behind.

Finally Boyd headed to the baseline, lifted a ball to show Gerry he was about to serve, and hit a missile. Gerry stepped around the body serve and sent a shot crosscourt, a clothesline shot that caught Boyd off-guard.

The comforting smell of toast wafted from the club, someone getting a last snack in the members' kitchen. Gerry thought, *Tennis. Nothing more. Nothing less.* A blessing. The widow was quiet, no longer rooting against him. Tears came to his eyes. She was all right. No, she wasn't. She would be. He willed his heart to slow down, a trick he'd learned when he was young and scared.

He had been seventeen when he got his first job in construction and didn't know what he was doing—there was the nailer skittering out of his hands and shooting a 3½-inch nail across his brow. He still had the scar. The time he fell off a roof at dusk, just as the last man was leaving the site.

Maybe he wouldn't survive the next hour of tennis. Maybe he'd drop from a heart attack. He turned his back to make Boyd wait for a second. Out of the light he could see stars, sharp tacks in the sky that appeared as if shot from a gun. They'd seen a lot of deaths. They didn't care.

This was what Kristy had not understood. It didn't matter how long she cried.

He blocked the next serve so it stopped and held in the air; Boyd lobbed it high. Anticipating the move, Gerry slid back and hit a perfect smash. He tried not to look at the widow but, against his will, saw her out of the corner of his eye, a statue with bowed head in the shadow, lost. He wanted to lift her up and yell at her, "Thanks for the tip! I'm going to win this thing. You made it happen!" Such a night. He wasn't himself. Usually he played quietly and steadily, as if doing a satisfying job. Luke was the kind to get worked up and use language, which the clubs frowned on. They acted like everyone still wore white flannels and bowed to the queen afterward.

He broke Boyd in that first game but lost the next three.

Gerry needed more sleep. He'd thought that for a while. A restlessness had come over him for months. He should stop working so much. At the first of the year, he'd hired three assistant managers, but one of them hadn't worked out, and the others needed a lot of guidance. Managing two small shopping centers—really just fancy strip malls with smoothie bars and blowout salons—wasn't that hard, but there was always something—plumbing, a patron crashing an SUV into signage, paperwork on the latest shoplifting charge. Gerry sometimes told the few women he dated that he was like a shark that couldn't afford to stop moving. He liked moving but hadn't figured out how to sleep. They'd laugh. He'd laugh. But lately he'd gotten the hollow feeling that he really couldn't slow down and someday would just swim off into the bay and through the Golden Gate and out into the vast bowl of scudding waves.

The widow started cheering for Boyd again. Dew made the balls skid off the lines, which should have been good for Gerry's power game, but his deep shots started to land long. Boyd sliced and diced his way to a lead. Gerry couldn't keep his mind on what was happening. What *was* happening?

His wife, Kristy, had burrowed into her sadness, deep down into the possibilities of sadness. Further than Gerry had ever been. After two months she said she couldn't stay with him.

"You could," he said. He felt like he was behind a door she'd locked; she tended a different world on her side.

"No," she said. "That's the problem. You don't understand. This—how I am today." She was standing in the kitchen. He'd just come home from picking up paint for the south side of the utility yard fence.

He put his hand on the granite counter. "Tomorrow will be different." If only she could see that.

"Look at me," she said. "What do you see?"

"Honestly?" She was trying to trap him.

She rolled her eyes.

"Someone who's gone too far." She was a mess. He wouldn't say that. "You don't have to let this happen," he said.

"That's what you don't understand. It happened. We don't have a choice."

"We always have a choice." She made him feel sullen, stupid.

"You're like talking to the wind."

He couldn't lose her. When they'd gotten married, he'd realized how far he'd come. She knew him as a successful guy. He'd just gotten the job at the first shopping center. He was good at logistics, details, holding together a large project. During the good times she'd put her arm through his and kiss the back of his neck. He needed that; he needed her. He vowed to grieve.

SCORE: 4-5. GERRY HAD to win the next serve to have a chance in the second set. He went over to the widow and said, "I know how you feel."

"I'm sure you do."

"I lost a son."

A flicker. A breath taken up in sympathy.

"Stillborn," he said, her raw face requiring truth.

That face shut down. "Stillborn." A pause. "You didn't wake up with him every morning, his chest against your back."

He said, "My wife left me."

She lifted her eyes again and sighed. "Do you think I care?"

"Be careful," he said, reeling. "You think that whatever you say now doesn't count but it does."

"Good. A lecture. What I need."

Her low voice was a weapon blowing holes in the night. How long had Gerry been living in silence?

"You should cheer for me," he said.

"I don't know you. I know Boyd. I've watched him before."

"I'm in your club."

"Sort of."

He felt cast out unfairly. So unfairly.

"You think I'm replacing him," he said, wanting to pierce her sadness.

"Luke," she said, her voice rising. "You should have said 'Luke.'" She turned her naked face to him, her eyes wild. "And keep your sick armchair whatever to yourself. He's dead. I'm not. And you're going to lose because Boyd knows how to push your buttons. There, how's that for some good armchair analysis."

"I'm not going to lose." Anger rose so quick and steep that he took a step back. He felt oddly useless, tongue-tied, so angry. He'd meant to bring her comfort. He went back to the court and won the next game.

When Kristy talked about separating, he took two weeks off and told her things would be different. He held her in his arms while she sighed and said she wondered if hope had been driven right out of her. He wanted to go to a café and drink coffee. Jog. In those days he jogged. Go to work. He vacuumed. Cleaned the kitchen until the granite needed to be resealed. Fixed her healthy meals and told her to eat.

He tried so hard to mourn, but a big, pulsing nothingness came over him when he thought of the awful hours he'd coached her to breathe as she gave birth to that bundle he'd seen in the nurse's arms. It was like a small, rubber turtle scrunched up against the nurse's flowered uniform. His little face looked powdered, bluish, not even as alive as a stuffed animal, just a cold, dead, folded thing. Or maybe he wasn't cold? The nurse held it out to him, but he said no, he didn't need that. She could wrap him up and take him away.

Instead she wrapped him up and gave him to Kristy to say good-bye.

Boyd won the second set.

The widow clapped. She went into the club. Maybe she'd leave. Then he could properly play for two, untarnished by her opposition. Play for Luke. Win for Luke! Put the night back together. Let the widow go blow up someone else with her awful sorrow.

Between sets Boyd lay down on his back on the court and pulled up one knee, then the other.

Good. Back trouble. All Gerry had to do was hit a few angles and make Boyd run. He'd been distracted and now everything seemed clear. Tomorrow had come, just as he'd predicted. He'd punched his way through. He was alive. Strong, the cooling night surging through his lungs. The widow was gone but her electric indifference fueled him. Poor Boyd, tightening up in the cool breeze.

Gerry took a deep, satisfying breath and served to start the deciding set. Boyd didn't get a point. Soon Gerry was up by a break.

The widow came back and took her seat. Gerry missed an easy volley and smashed his racket on the ground like a junior. The frame cracked and he had to get his second racket from his bag. As he went to the bench, the widow said, "See, ego."

Furious, he leaped halfway up the mound before stopping himself. What was he going to do? Hit her? "What did you say?"

"I said, ego. Your undoing."

"Why are you doing this to me?"

"No reason. Something to do. Better than killing someone." She was calm, becalmed, a sailor on a flat sea dying of thirst.

He went back to the courts and played some of the best tennis of his life. Yet Boyd hung on, coming to the net and finishing points early to save his back. They got to a seven-point tiebreaker to decide the match.

Gerry calmly walked up to her before they started and quietly asked, "Would you go home now? Please. Leave me to my fate?"

"Just when things were getting interesting?" But even

as she said it, a look crossed her face. "I sleep on the floor," she said. A long pause. "With the boogeymen. I can't sleep in the bed. My goddaughter gave me her camping pad." A piece of hair got loose from the clip and crossed her face. She tucked it behind her ear, then reached up and took his hand in both of hers. "You've given me two hours and seven minutes." She shook his hand, as if they'd just agreed on something. "Thank you."

"Thank you," he said because that seemed right. He turned and walked back slowly, a great ease coming over him. Boyd served and Gerry cracked the return up the line, but Boyd somehow got it and dinked a winner just over the net.

The widow cheered for Boyd.

Gerry smiled. He played well and got up 5-2. Easy. He just had to hold his nerve. The automatic lights went out on the farthest court, bringing the darkness closer. And in that instant he remembered one terrible moment. Kristy had said that she'd spent eight months talking to their son, telling him what she was doing—"Now I'm sitting on the porch. Now I'm folding the wash." She said she wanted him to know how things worked before he arrived so he'd be competent at existence. This was why she couldn't say good-bye so fast.

"It doesn't help to be sentimental," he'd said. Oh no, he hadn't said that. He had. On the tennis court his cheeks burned with shame. He'd wanted to wound her, punish her for leaving their old life behind long before he'd even known she was gone. Pregnant, she'd already turned her back on him and faced the slow-moving miracle. She was lost in awe, lost to him. He hadn't known.

It was his serve but he stood without moving. He was the one who couldn't go forward, before or after the death.

A ship of some kind gave a short blast of its horn, then the resounding quiet. Across the court Boyd swayed back and forth, waiting. The widow was quiet. She slept on the floor. Gerry served a wobbly thing that caught Boyd off-guard and so he missed.

The rest of the tiebreak was a blur. Then Boyd was shaking his hand. "Not fair," he said good-naturedly. "I'm the one who wins with junk." Boyd packed up quickly. "Got to get home and get the wife to ice my back." He left.

She was still there. "You won," she said. A faint smile. "Fucker."

He sat down. The chair was icy. "Fuck you too."

Silence. The lights clicked off on Court 6. She said quietly, "Fuck you and the horse you came in on."

He said, "Such a fucking horse."

More silence. Not looking at him, she nodded and got up. "Thanks again. I have to go home. Don't want my goddaughter to call the search team." She started down the little grassy hill and then turned back. "Have a good life." Then she was gone.

There he was on a cold chair. Her scent was more like a memory. He didn't have anyone to talk to, which was OK—he had nothing to say. No stories to instruct someone on how to exist. His surging blood was slowing, and soon the sweat in his T-shirt would cool, encasing him in cold fabric. He needed a hot shower. He needed to change something but didn't know what. His life. Everything. How did he get so far in the hole so fast? He didn't move.

Into his mind came a story. A month after his fall at the construction site, he was on the roof again. The foreman had told him that afternoon that he had a good work ethic and would take him off probation. He had the job. There was sun on the new shingles. The smell of wood. The other guys were packing their trucks.

He stepped out on the spine of the roof. He was a tight-rope walker two-and-a-half stories up into the sky. At the far edge he bent and grasped the gable with his hands, then lifted his legs into a handstand. The world went upside down. The neighbor's roof was wrong, strange. Exquisite terror swept through him. He corrected his balance with his legs. Corrected again. His arms shook, his strength ebbing. He stayed one beat longer, holding on, letting his terror ripple down into the house they were building. Then, finally, he lowered his legs and made sure he had traction before setting his weight down.

No one had seen. He wished someone had seen. He couldn't tell the others—they were family men and risks were stupid. Soon he forgot.

Gerry realized that the traffic sounds had died, and he could hear the waves in the bay, a restless sound that didn't comfort. Have a good life. A throwaway line. After all these years he still had no one to tell the story. He should have remembered and told Kristy. She was a good listener. She would have tilted her head and said, "Oh, I wonder why you did that." He wondered alone. And as he wondered, his heart slowed. The cold dew felt somehow nourishing. It would help grow new courts, new nets, all new in the morning. He'd have to find someone to tell his story. Or not. That handstand was his. His slice of sweet, holy terror. Unseen. His life.

ATLANTIS

An invitation to the Todhunters' party had come in the mail before the separation. As Adrienne and Mark dressed for the party in their own rooms, he tried hard to remember why he let her talk him into going. Would they just pretend she wasn't pregnant by another man?

Outrage overwhelmed Mark. He sat on the bed crammed against the wall. Their cottage in Palo Alto had once been the carriage house for the mansion next door. Adrienne had hung an oval mirror beside the closet to make the bedroom look bigger. Mark touched his jaw. His eyes were almost black, sunken against his pale skin, pasty now. From a distance of ten feet away you would think he hadn't slept, though every night he dropped heavily into dreams of falling.

He'd often imagined a boy—or a girl, he didn't care—holding his hand and asking how a car worked or where the water in the tap came from. For 16 barren years, he'd held this image of a child. The sex was timed. There were humiliating tests. His sperm wriggled on a slide under the magnified eye of a bored technician. Doctor Kronberger had said there was no physical reason he and Adrienne couldn't have a baby. For months, they had hardly touched. Mark had been engulfed by the dry ambiguity of the exams, the sense that something had failed besides biology.

One night before going to bed in the extra room that had been a porch, Adrienne stood in the living room and said very quietly, "You've never seen the father. We could pretend he never existed. He doesn't want to have anything to do with this. I can't go to my deathbed without knowing what it's like to love a child. I'll die of bitterness."

"Either you will or I will." The newspaper on Mark's lap told of starvation in Sudan, glaciers calving into the sea, malware corrupting nuclear plants.

She nodded. "You were desperate for a baby," she said.

"How dare you mention that!" He threw the paper across the room. The giant fan palms lining the neighbor's driveway cast night shadows on the carpet.

With shaking hands, Mark buttoned the cuffs of his shirt. He would be 40 next year. More than halfway there. The faint figure of a vine in the wallpaper—green on green—seemed to spell out his loneliness. He could hear the rustle of Adrienne moving across the hall. She stood in the doorway in a loose, red dress with a cotton jacket. She looked almost as skinny and leggy as before.

"No one could tell," he said.

"Good. We can just go. Not think."

THE TODHUNTERS LIVED ON Magdalena Avenue where it wound into the Los Altos hills above Palo Alto. Their house looked like two large shelves jutting off the rocky slope. Cece and Charles Todhunter had been Mark's acquaintances for some time and, recently, his clients. The Todhunters had one son, Rob, now 15. Mark helped them set up their estate as a trust fund for Rob's children, if he ever had any. The boy was, in a sense, cut out of their will.

Rob stood at the doorway taking summer coats. He had sleepy eyes, baby cheeks, and a smile that held the trace of a sneer. He said "Greetings," threw their coats in slow-motion exuberance over his arm, and took them to a bedroom down the hall to his right.

Cece came through the guests crowded into the expansive, marble-floored entry and took Mark's and Adrienne's hands in hers. "So glad you could come," she said a little breathlessly. She had short, stiff hair, earrings like little plates, spangled top. With a frown, she watched Rob go out the propped-open door, then she turned back and spoke to Adrienne. "I haven't seen you at the gym for a while. Someone said you were in Europe."

Adrienne smiled and lied, "Long trip. Sweden is so Sweden. Great to be home."

A sound burst over the crowd cocktail chatter. Gunshot? Backfire? Cece gave a start.

"I'll see what's happening." Her top shimmered. "'Scuse me." She trotted quickly out the front door and down the steps to a battered BMW that was just pulling up to the walkway.

The car seemed to burst with teenagers, their arms and someone's bare foot out the windows. One girl leaned through the front passenger's window as she called for Rob. The boy walked across the stone steps, clapping his hands. "Reinforcements. All right."

"I told you," said his mother as she reached for his shoulder, "no friends." A floodlight beamed up into a cherry tree beside her. "Not tonight," she said fervently to her son. "This is *my* party."

In the entry, someone in a bow tie brought wine on a tray. Mark took two glasses, giving one to Adrienne to hold. She hadn't had a drop of caffeine or alcohol for a month. Mark had always thought that he was the disciplined one. "Cece told me," he said to Adrienne, speaking directly into her ear to be heard above the clamor, "that Rob got kicked out of St. Francis." This was a private school in town, known for its high academics, a brutally successful football team. "He plagiarized his English papers off the Internet. Charles is sick about it."

"Let's not talk about them while we're in their house."

"They can't hear." The pregnancy made her infuriatingly high-minded, remote.

She looked at him. "You're saying what they don't know can't hurt them."

"They already know." He almost choked on his own sulkiness.

They edged their way across the room and up a broad staircase, finding themselves at a glass door embedded in a row of floor-to-ceiling windows that looked out on a deck. "Let's go out," Mark said. "I'm suffocating."

There was a space in the crowd, and they found their way to the outer edge of the deck. It was encircled by a steel rail that seemed to be holding the crowd back from spilling into thin air. Adrienne put a hand on the rail as the breeze lifted strands of hair across her forehead. Her fragrance, like the clean smell of smooth stones, spread over Mark. He quickly drank both glasses of wine, placed them on the tray held by a young man with dyed black hair, and took two flutes of champagne. Discreet outdoor lights shone across the crowd in the balmy night air and lit up the long steel bars that connected the deck's glass roof to its slate floor. Adrienne seemed to sparkle. Holding another life. Ready to launch.

Mark had met her at Santa Clara University when she was a freshman. They often talked for hours under the eucalyptus trees. The campus, with its Mexican mission and hundred-year-old roses, had lulled Mark into a longing for something he couldn't describe. In the 18th century, Franciscan padres had walked to Santa Clara from Mexico. Walked a thousand miles. They must have been as lonely as men could get, but something drove them.

Mark wondered what he and Adrienne had talked about. Now, their tense conversations contained so little, often just a dry jokiness that left Mark feeling old. He remembered one Friday after classes when they drove all night to Mexico in his beat-up Volvo. They didn't come back for three weeks. His grades dropped, he almost flunked out and ruined his chances for law school next year. He didn't care. With her, he was invincible.

The Todhunters' very small, irregular swimming pool 20 feet below sent the smell of wet concrete up through the surrounding trees. The pool was decorative, more like an artfully placed puddle in the landscape. Mark took Adrienne's hand on the rail. She didn't pull away. "I never asked you how you feel," he said.

"You're asking now?" Her pale lashes gleamed in the floodlight. "That's bad."

He was drowning. He couldn't figure out which way was up to get air. "I mean physically," he said. "You don't seem sick."

"No. Some women aren't. I'm in the lucky ten percent."

"You don't feel anything?"

"I feel everything." She looked down at the undersized

pool. Lights in the water threw green shadows against the surrounding bushes and boulders. A young girl in jeans and halter top sat on one of the boulders. The girl from the car. Cece bent down beside her, as if they were in heated conversation.

Adrienne said, "Not exactly a heartbeat, but a swelling sensation that starts behind my ribs and seems to flood my belly, then pull back."

He couldn't speak.

She said, "I didn't think you wanted to know." She turned his hand and smoothed his fingers. "It's hard to describe. It's like the baby is tugging on me. Even this early."

"We could have been happy," he said.

She lifted her eyes. "Don't say that." The whites of her eyes were milky above that damned red dress.

There was a commotion behind her. She turned, her throat creamy in the light. Mark looked up. Rob had hopped up onto the rail and was standing on it, one hand grasping one of the long poles leading to the roof. The boy wore a baggy flowered swimsuit. His bare knees, so square, looked vulnerable. His white chest, plump with the last of his baby fat, seemed incongruous with his big feet and full, open mouth. He seemed to be drinking in the night, considering his chances. Mark wondered where the other kids were. The crowd began to quiet as guests realized what Rob was doing.

Far below, Cece shouted, "No!" She lifted her hands, a small pleading figure.

Rob jumped. For a long moment, he seemed to descend slowly through the air, his feet bicycling as if he were trying to climb back up to the balcony, his white shoulders like wings as he passed from balcony lights to garden beams. On his face was a stiff smile of horror, and then there was a splash. A splash! No blood on the rocks. Mark was amazed. Like an acrobat diving into a barrel. Rob was a body in the green water, swimming three strokes to the side, and then he emerged and became a boy again as he took a huge intake of breath. He yelled to the girl, "You owe me twenty bucks. Pay up." He hoisted himself to the pebbly pavement and came dripping to the girl, his suit clinging to him.

A strange excitement seized Mark. "They're babies," he said to Adrienne, "and then they grow up."

She shook her head in the sudden silence and leaned intently over the rail, her thoughts hidden from him.

Below, Cece emerged from the shadows. "You don't have to do this," she hissed to her son. Her voice rang across the water and rose through the hush of the crowd. "Please," Cece said. "OK. Just go with them." She shook her head in disgust. "One night. That was all—"

"I told you in the first place," said her son fiercely. "You shouldn't have forced me to come." He ducked his head as if dismayed at what he'd done, but unable to stop.

Mark took Adrienne's shoulder, so smooth in the silky dress. He wanted to prod her, make her wince with fury like his. "Do you really want to end up alone with a kid?" he whispered.

"Not alone," she said calmly. She drew back. "If I can help it."

She was unmovable, certain of her desires. Irrationally, Mark longed for the unbearable thrill of seeing the boy drop through the air again. *Encore!* he thought crazily. Anything to jar Adrienne out of her queenliness. Where were the other kids? Weren't they challenged by this feat?

No, Rob was hulking off alone along the path to the garage, and the other kids seemed to have disappeared.

Mark found the wide stairway that led down to the little pool house, took off his shoes on the musty wood slats. Shirt on or off? Irrationally, he rolled up the sleeves. Underwater champ at the Paly Y. Three laps in the big pool. He and his high school friends permanently banned after the last World Aquaman Championship.

He felt light as he crossed the cool grit of the pool apron. A few guests watched idly as he slipped under the surface. They'd see his bubbles. The trail of Aquaman. A shudder of cold. But wait, he forgot something. Not much in the tank. His steady kick, but the tug of starvation already in his lungs. He should have hyperventilated. In the locker room when no one saw. A wall loomed. No space to flip. A few more kicks and another wall. Such a tiny pool. Aquaman suffocating. The muffled thunk of a rescue guard device. He stopped and sculled to stay deep, his chest dragging for air, head splitting. He gave a mighty kick. Grabbed the cylinder with both hands. Gasped, wild gasping. An animal unto itself. Air hurt. Lights blasting with salt, chlorine.

The guests were black shapes under the trees, leaning toward him, curious. Cece looked down at him, her streaked face set, her eyes smudged with makeup. "Why did you do that?" she asked grimly. "Why did you scare us like that? This is what he wants. Disruption. Chaos. You, a grown man. *Stunt* man."

Intense sheepishness overcame Mark. He could almost breathe. How long since he'd been scolded? He wanted to smile foolishly, shrug elaborately, and say he was sorry. Between breaths, he lifted his eyebrows at Cece. She shook her head, turned, and threw the rope to the device in the water.

Now what? Did he go dripping to the car? He felt like he was inside a cool envelope, his face and shoulders touched by the balmy summer air. Maybe he'd just float around on his back for a while. Or would his clothes sink him?

Adrienne appeared on the lower deck. She leaned over him. "Now that was mature," she said, her voice hoarse with anger. Water shadows danced across her face.

"I wanted to feel like a kid." And something else he couldn't explain. The thrill of thinking he'd lost everything. He found a small ladder in the water and put his foot on the bottom rung. His clothes swam around him.

"You had this sudden urge to humiliate yourself?" she asked grimly.

He thought about that. "Maybe." He pulled himself out. He felt shrink-wrapped in his shirt and pants. Something very funny seemed to be budding inside him. "Maybe I was trying it on for size."

She gave a snort, kept her distance from his wet self. "I'll just pretend I don't know you," she said, but then her face changed and a slight smile flitted through her eyes.

He leaned forward and kissed her, and she brushed the drips off her face and laughed.

MARK THOUGHT HIS SWIM would cure something or make something clearer, but it didn't. He was merely left with the longing to be young and reckless again. He felt defiant somehow. Standing at the large window of his fourth-floor office in downtown Palo Alto, he was more aware of the teenagers who swaggered down University Avenue, the girls with hibiscus tops, the strutting boys. He wanted to be like they were, carelessly fecund, not conscious of their motives but only of their pounding hearts.

When he and Adrienne were first married, he had told her funny stories about the foibles of his clients, the ones who changed their wills every few months, as if in deep, after-death combat with their relatives. One wanted his niece assigned as guardian to his son. The son was 43. Mark told Adrienne that he felt like his job was to organize death. If the client dies on Thursday, we will do this, go this way. If he dies on Tuesday, we will go over there, that way. The plans made him feel helpless and self-important at once. How could he have been so sentimental?

Friday morning, his longtime client Mrs. Janice Eaton McKenzie came to his office without an appointment. She was over 90. She wore a suit with braided piping and little square shoulders and walked carefully into his office, bent, watching the carpet for obstacles, not speaking. The freckled folds of her downturned face seemed to cling not to bone, but to fine wires that held her together.

Mark fought his impatience. Mrs. McKenzie and her husband had been some of his first clients. She'd tolerated his novice mistakes, cheerily stopping by the office to sign papers he had overlooked. Mark had thought of her almost as his grandmother and had been disturbed to hear about her decline when her daughter and then her husband died.

In his heightened state, her frailty seemed almost like an affront. Her husband had been dead a year. At first, she'd refused to take Mark's calls. Her son said she wasn't accepting the death very well. She even sent back her first dividend checks. Six months later, the son said she'd quit eating, and Mark wondered if he was going to lose her. He marveled at her refusal to let go of her husband. She scared him a little. He couldn't dismiss her. Most of the very old meekly let him herd them through the rituals of crossing over.

Finally, she looked up at him and adjusted her frail mouth to speak. Her hooded eyes made half-moons of her pupils. Outside the window behind her head, a jet reeled out a contrail. "I'm better," she said without preliminaries.

Gratefulness flooded through him. He put both hands on his desk, which seemed wide and generous. So. She wasn't lost. He could hardly believe it. On her own, without his guiding hand, she'd shuffled her way back from grief. Outside, the blue sky seemed to dive down upon the trees and houses below. The contrail puffed and then faded in a wind blowing high above the still town. "I'm glad to hear that," he said quickly. Hollow words. There was so much more to say! "I mean, I'm glad you came to tell me that.

She smiled, and the wrinkles took new places, a brilliant scattering. "Time heals," she said. "Even at my age."

WHEN SHE LEFT, MARK walked home quickly. He had to do something, break this impasse. Adrienne said that she hadn't set out to get pregnant, hadn't set out to do anything. What happened just happened. She'd broken up with her lover after only a month. It was a big mistake. Her will was no more than that of a spore drifting to the ground, seeking heat. What about the time at dawn after an argument when they'd walked on the wooden path leading into the baylands marsh? The wind beat against their coats and hair as they turned and clutched each other. Another time, she brought daffodils to his office, found a vase in the coffee room, and as she ran water, he slipped a hand under her blouse and she laughed, and for one moment, he felt the flutter of her self beating against his palm. Just for him. Just for him! He walked into the still, vacant house. It seemed disappointingly emptied of their history. His chair stood near the window. His row of law books on the shelf were dust.

Adrienne's lover had been a tenant in one of the apartment buildings she managed south of town. He was an electrician. The baby would have the electrician's eyes, nose, mouth. No. Mark had demanded details. The guy's name was Stewart Prince. What kind of name was that for the father of his wife's baby? So mincing and lacking in seriousness. Adrienne said that Stewart moved to L.A. after the breakup. L.A.! Wasn't that a place for wannabes? Actors and producers. A wannabe electrician.

He had to find some sort of evidence. Did Adrienne joke with him the way she did with Mark? Were there love letters? His heart dropped. Movie stubs? Did she go to the movies with him when Mark worked late? Or did they just want sex? Did she do it in a position that Stewart wanted, arching and talking dirty like she used to with Mark? Was there a place on her that he touched that Mark had never found? Did she buy him presents? Were there unusual charges on her credit card bills that Mark barely glanced through? He had to get his hands on their connection, see its shape, what it did to her.

Since Adrienne had confessed, she'd been scrupulous about telling him her schedule, and he knew that she had a meeting at noon with her painting crew at the apartments to discuss new colors for a vacant end unit. He went to the spare room and rummaged through the pockets of her clothes hanging in the narrow closet. A sense of doom thrilled through him.

Outside, pale sprouts furred clods of earth in the garden.

Adrienne hadn't had time to plant flowers this year. Mark carefully lifted her folded sweaters from the shelf above the hangers. The porch had a pleasantly astringent, weedy smell. Adrienne had pulled the coverlet smoothly over the bed. He turned in her tidy room, sensing her sanctuary, a place he couldn't enter no matter how long he stood there. He opened drawers in the small bureau. At least there should be a scrap of paper with the electrician's new address. Nothing under her lingerie. She'd cleaned her lover out of her life.

He went to the alcove near the kitchen that she used for her office and rifled through her files. There was one marked *Forwarding*. Yes, there on a 3 × 5 card, printed in large, looping handwriting, not Adrienne's: Stewart Prince, 4 Wisteria Lane, Santa Monica. The flowing letters seemed to shout at him. Look what I took from you. See, you'll never feel at ease again!

The next morning, Saturday, Mark told Adrienne that something had come up, he had to work all day, and that he'd see her for a late dinner at about 10. To his surprise, the lie came easily. He'd thought she was the liar. Then he took a commuter flight from San Jose to LAX. The cabbie knew the street, and soon, Mark was standing on the doorstep of a stucco house surrounded by some kind of citrus bushes with shiny leaves. A Toyota with a paint job faded to pink stood in the driveway. Mark knocked on the door. A tall boy answered almost immediately, the glare from the sun obscuring his features.

"I'm looking for Stewart Prince," Mark said. He pictured a paunchy guy with a patronizing smile.

"The same," said the boy. He backed up and motioned Mark to come in.

Him? How could that be? Mark could feel himself

moving from brightness to the cool dark of the room. His head felt too light to balance. "I could be a burglar." He wanted to sound menacing.

Stewart shrugged, unafraid. He wore shorts, no shirt, and had the soft muscles of a natural athlete. "You don't look like a burglar."

"I'm Adrienne's husband."

Stewart gave a start. He took a breath through flared nostrils. "She sent you?"

"No." Mark's eyes began to adjust, and there before him was an approximation of his own face when he was younger. The black eyes and pale skin. The hefty nose. There were some differences, heavier brows and a chin more square—the boy was not a relative, but the wide bones and resemblance of coloring were striking.

Stewart saw it too. "Whoa," he breathed.

Mark turned. "You must be my lost twin." He felt like he was chirping silly quips. He wanted to show strength, *gravitas*, but the habit of cutting off his thoughts was too strong.

"She knows her taste," Stewart said seriously.

Mark winced. He had seen this phenomenon of likeness in friends and clients who'd gone through bitter divorces, then turned around and married someone remarkably similar in build or temperament or quality of voice. His college roommate married three Nancys. "How old are you?' he asked.

"Twenty-six and counting."

Mark felt a little surge of pride that Adrienne was able to attract someone so young. "Could I sit down?"

"If you're not going to shoot me." A little smile.

MARK RECOGNIZED HIS OWN speedy assessment of a

situation, the quick hiding of the heart. The likeness was psychological as well as physical. Maybe Adrienne was seeking Mark himself. She'd strayed toward him. Maybe.

A couch stood at right angles to the plaster fireplace rimmed in green tile. A little bit of Spanish style. A pleasant room. A table stood against a rounded window. The table was covered with sketches, and there was a colored picture on a pad propped on a music stand. Mark pushed a pillow aside. "I don't know why I came here."

"To know the enemy?" The boy sat in the rattan chair. He was calm now, as if he met his lovers' husbands every day.

Yes. Was there a moment when this boy and Adrienne held back against the silences gathering between them? Then, did they kiss anyway? Or did they go after each other without thinking? "Did you paint that?" Mark motioned to the picture on the stand.

Stewart nodded. "It's not paint, it's pastel." Two pencil lines about three inches apart crossed the width of the paper, like two horizons. Fitted between the lines were several sailboats heeling over so far that the tops of their masts almost touched the water. They looked like they were at the edge of the earth in an ancient map.

"It's good," Mark said. Sitting with the man who'd fucked his wife, he felt a sense of anticipation. There'd been an earthquake at Santa Clara once, and just before the coffee cups started to rattle, Mark sensed a deep pause, a death.

"She encouraged me to keep sketching," Stewart said. "And she made me fill out the application for UCLA. I've gone back to school."

"As an artist?"

"Architect. Drawing's on the side." There was a pause. "I've always wanted to do this. I'm happy."

A strange thing to say, "happy," with the same certainty as knowing you were, say, thirsty. How long since Mark had felt so sure? In a flash, he sensed that Adrienne hadn't told Stewart about the baby. "I have to go," he said.

"Just when we were having fun." That quick, easy smile.

Now Mark saw it. The liaison had been a lark for Stewart. He looked at it as a pleasant sidestep on the way to a future that would solidify into some sort of glory. His heart hadn't been blasted with the sameness of days and then, when you least expected, the mad bursts of grief over what was gone. Mark didn't shake Stewart's hand or try for words of farewell. "See you around," he said.

"Yeah, right." The boy turned. "Listen. I didn't mean to hurt you."

Mark needed to escape. He flung open the door. "I understand. I wasn't part of the equation. Not everything works out the way you want." He fled down the concrete stairs. Now here. Now gone.

He walked fast down the street as if he had someplace to go. Low, stucco houses with air conditioners attached to side windows and scrubby lawns stood beside the cracked sidewalk. A rental district. On one roof was a sofa next to an oversized umbrella.

There was a coffee shop two blocks down. Not Starbucks, a place with BLTs and bad coffee. Mark sat at the Formica counter. Maybe he was hungry. Two o'clock. Had he eaten breakfast? He asked the waitress with candy-white hair for a French dip and ate it slowly, soaking each crumb in surprisingly savory broth. Could have been homemade. The waitress was old enough to be his mother. He ate the pickled apple on the side. His mother had died his last year of high school. He and his father rattled around in their sprawling house near the Redwood City harbor. His father told him to take whatever things of hers he wanted. Mark didn't know what to keep. Not her jewelry; it should stay with his father. Not her bedside stand. Not the old-fashioned figurines of cute kids with puppies that embarrassed him when his friends came over. All her things were too female, too filled with grief. In the end he took nothing, and his father, panicked with loneliness, gave almost everything to Goodwill.

Mark nursed a cup of coffee for hours. The waitress didn't mind. Two women in their early twenties came in and sat whispering in a booth beside him. They crossed their legs and slouched forward, their skinny backs curved so Mark could see the little bulges of their vertebrae just above their hips] They were talking about getting high. He thought of Rob Todhunter, stoned, free-falling. Aquaman sinking below the surface. Was that the last time he'd been happy? He paid his bill and asked quietly as he passed the girls, "Can you hook me up?" He went outside and stood by the vending bins of newspapers. This was stupid. Even if they were, they wouldn't connect with a glassy-eyed mer-man in a Polo shirt and tassle loafers.

They did come out. The one with pigtails and a whale tattoo on her biceps said, "You want something?"

"A joint." He tried to sound gruff. The cinder block wall of the restaurant held a little pink from the sunset. Darkness was falling fast.

The girl's very red mouth moved into a contemptuous smile. "I'll need a note from your doctor." She giggled. "We don't serve them wrapped, Mister. Not like in your day, I guess."

"But I don't have any papers." *Stop pleading.*

"All right," said her companion, stepping in. She wore a short skirt over leggings.

He fished in his pocket for the bills, and they left, bumping playfully into each other, softly hooting.

At least the joint was substantial. Mark stood in the shadows by the garbage shed and smoked it fast, choking, the glow bobbing in the growing darkness. He thought of a joke he'd heard of a drunken driver getting stopped. The policeman asked him why he was speeding. "Well, sir," said the man, "I knew I wasn't driving so good so I wanted to get home fast." A sense of wholeness came over Mark. He felt himself join some sort of grand scheme. Now he was pinching out the end of the joint burning close to his lips. Now he was eating the remnant, swallowing some kind of secret.

He must have missed something about Stewart and Adrienne, some piece of the puzzle that would tell him how to feel. He walked back to Stewart's house. The Toyota was gone. He let himself into the side yard. Very quietly so the neighbors wouldn't hear, he pulled up the purple hibiscus, a clump of small daisies, and two young citrus bushes. He was surprised at his strength against the roots in clay earth. He carefully dumped the garbage can. Rinds of oranges and chicken bones rolled into the dirt. He found a pair of garden shears propped on the fence cross-bar and nosed through the garbage. Didn't Stewart start a sketch for Adrienne and then crumple it into the refuse, or write her a letter he never sent, or something? Mark was an anthropologist searching for meaning in the middens of the city. Hadn't Stewart left *some* evidence? Oh yes, by the way, his cells. Mark cut the hose into three parts, then put the shears in his pocket. The sliding glass door was locked. He tried the laundry room window. Locked, but the bathroom window at the side yard was cracked. He lifted it, old paint flaking into his hands. He leaned in, closed the toilet seat with outstretched hand, eased down and into the bathroom. Breaking and entering. Well, not exactly breaking. He gave a hard laugh. *Sh*, he told himself. He laughed again. Mustn't leave fingerprints. If he moved fast, maybe they wouldn't stick. He flicked Motrin, sunscreen, toothpaste out on the floor. He went into the front room and used the shears to punch a hole in the sailboat. He emptied the drawer of a desk. Rubber bands, paper clips, a protractor, a roll of cash, a box of pens, stamps, and scissors fell out. He stabbed the couch with the shears and ripped the corduroy, knocked over the lamp, shattered a framed painting in the hall. *He* would leave evidence for Stewart. Stewart would not forget *him*.

He walked out the front and went back to the restaurant. The waitress was vacuuming, but she let him sit at the counter. The neon sign for beer behind the milk shake machine seemed a sympathetic green. The restaurant was a lighted tent against the hot night. Mark called a Lyft on his cell.

His house was ablaze with lights under a full moon. Adrienne's emptied closet stood open, hangers at angles. Mark felt the swooping doom of someone in a race who realizes that another runner is just about to pass him. He turned off all the lights except the kitchen. A welter of stars was caught in the gauze of the Milky Way. Mark thought of distant explosions so immense that new worlds were made and destroyed. How could this be? Mark couldn't sit. Couldn't stand. The dim patio light was still on. There was Adrienne on her knees in the garden, a flat of nasturtiums at her side. He walked out the side door. She was a dark figure hunched in the flower bed in front of a row of giant ferns.

She looked up. Shadows fell across her eyes. "Memorial flowers to remember me by." She gave a small smile.

He sank to his knees beside her. Gently, he said, "You're planting by Braille?" They'd always joked.

She smiled, then straightened up, her hand on her belly. He could see that she hadn't changed her mind. "I realized I didn't need daylight to dig them in," she said. "They're not fussy. Just need a clump of soil and a little water. They're almost weeds." With her fingers, she pressed dirt against one of the orange-flowered plants.

The palms cast long shadows across the patio. The rooms of the dark house were haunted with furniture shapes. Mark realized that a chance likeness made a secret possible. He wouldn't have to tell his child anything until later. The child could grow up in carefree ignorance. He would know his home. Facts could come later. That wouldn't be fair, but it was possible.

"Did I ever tell you," he asked, "about Mrs. McKenzie?"

Adrienne put her hands on the thighs of her jeans and watched him.

"She's ninety-two," Mark said. Telling this right was critical. Ferns touched his shoulders and made his heart beat fast. "Her husband died a year ago. I saw her yesterday, and she felt like talking. She told me all her friends are dead. Her only daughter died at seventy-three of a heart attack. Her son lives in Florida. She said most people her age felt like they'd lived their lives and they were ready for the end. Wished for it." He felt like he had to carry the story in all its fidelity directly to Adrienne.

The tips of the palm shadows brushed the windows of the house. Mark's mind turned. Or maybe he would tell his child everything and face the wrenching legal hassle of custody and questions. Rely on exposed truth to forge the way. Imagine. He went on quickly. "Mrs. McKenzie said, 'I can hardly walk. I can barely see. My stomach won't take most foods. But I want to wake up in the morning. Isn't that something? I've outlived reason.'" The wet earth had soaked through the knees of his suit pants.

Adrienne didn't move. She seemed like the only steady being in the gentle storm of swaying plants. She brushed her hands clean on her jeans. She started to say something, stopped. Then said softly, "I vowed to leave before you got home."

"But you didn't," he said quickly.

"No. I kept procrastinating, postponing the moment—" She looked at him. The ferns were their shelter, murmuring, uncurling with life. She took his hand and moved it to the belly of her T-shirt. He felt a slight stir. Maybe. The dew was just beginning to sift out of the night.

He closed his eyes. The darkness yielded nothing. He looked at Adrienne. Her face was white in the moonlight. She reached up and touched his cheek.

He leaned into her palm, raising his shoulder. "I thought you were gone," he breathed. "I didn't know what to do."

"I just kept staying and staying." She looked at him. The breeze carried a touch of the cool night yet to come. She moved closer to his side.

"My suitcases are in my car," she said.

With the weight of her against him, his heart slowed. Her hair was silk on his cheek. He gazed up into the night.

SLIDE IT CLOSER TO THE CENTER

or no reason, Bobbie's loneliness lifted a little, like the day a flu starts to ebb and you hear a bird. The Seattle day was windy and bright. She pulled on her denim.

Her worktable ran the length of the spare room, holding parts for mobiles she sold at Pike Place. In one corner lay a pile of unfinished miniature wire bicycles and, in another, gorgeous purple Lady Gaga fishing flies that looked oddly stranded when hung. More projects sat in plastic bins on shelves. Since Tomas had left, the parts had felt like clumsy, sentimental detritus. They weighed her down. He had promised to bring his granddaughter Starlyn by for a visit the first Monday of every month. A silversmith, Tomas still delivered his custom men's rings, conchos and fancy bridles to Shilshole Saddles in person— on time and beautiful. Bobbie had ached for him through three long Mondays. Three times, he hadn't shown.

Another first Monday. She turned on the work light. *They will not come.* This was true. They'd had two years together, now done. She was forty-four, alone again, married only briefly at nineteen, childless. But ready. She smiled. For something.

She pulled her high stool up to the bicycles. They didn't look so heavy as she remembered. She'd used needle-nosed pliers to bend them into shape, and the striations from the tool added texture. She set to work adding more spokes to the wheels of the racing bike for a look of speed.

Tomas had taken Starlyn to Butte, Montana, his hometown, for her to grow up in a purer atmosphere away from traffic on all the bridges, the Seattle freeze stare, almond double mocha lattes with friggin' swizzle art, CEOs clogging up the decent bars, tourists. Ha! Butte had tourists! Bobbie had seen a photo in Wikipedia. Tourists leaning over a rail at a poisoned mine in the center of Butte. She continued snipping sturdy wire. Bobbie once took Starlyn to lunch at Lowell's, climbing the steps to the third floor, eating in silence as layers of fog settled over the Sound, making ferries disappear. "Wow," Starlyn had whispered. Montana was landlocked, for God's sake.

A SEPTEMBER MORNING OF sunshine dazzling the ripple of incoming tide at the foot of the market. Bobbie stood at her Saturday spot in the crafts pavilion. The mobiles were hung on two clothesline displays. Locals and tourists surged down the main aisle. Laughing, talking, handling merchandise, moving on. Five teenagers bumping into each other. Women in Hello Kitty! sweatshirts, arms linked. A tall guy about her age—salt-and-pepper ponytail, collared shirt—half-trotting past the dahlia vendor, calling "Starling, Starling!"

A girl, maybe seven, appeared alone at Bobbie's table.

"I want to buy your cheapest one," she said, gazing up at

the mobiles dangling miniature kites, little hammers and saws, Space Needles and MoPops and coho salmon (her best-seller). Bobbie said, "Do you have a financier?"

She thought through the word. "No."

Bobbie pointed out the one with a *Moby Dick* novel as big as a large postage stamp dangling next to a dictionary, a Sebastian Berry epic, another by Hanya Yanagihara. She tapped a text to security to find the frantic man with the ponytail. "Do you like books?" she asked the girl.

"Sometimes." She wore a pink t-shirt, a worn friendship bracelet, shorts, rainboots despite the weather. She didn't smile. Loneliness clung to her hands at her sides.

"I call these my Book Mobiles." The joke was lost on her.

Ponytail appeared next to the child's side, catching his breath. Security waved from the next aisle and left.

"These don't look like bracelets." He smiled at the kid, beads of sweat on his narrow forehead.

"I'd like one of these," she said solemnly, moving close to him, not quite touching. He took a breath. They were planets orbiting each other.

Bobbie got a lot of divorced fathers, trying hard, weekend visiting. She said, "Maybe Dad could take you to my friend's shop. Jade bracelets. River rock. Some of my pieces are there. You could decide."

She fingered the Husky balanced against a Dawg house and a bone. "Not Da-*d*," she said matter-of-factly. "Just Da. Dad is at Spokane Community this semester." She looked at Bobbie. "This time, he's not playing."

"A serious student."

She shrugged, thinking. "Mo-*m* is dead. He tried. But he has a future, too."

Bobbie asked her neighbor Daniel—knitted socks and caps—to cover, and took them to Bette's Space in the Post

Alley, then on to the Pink Door for tea with décor matching Starlyn's tee. The child smiled at that, a first. Her grandfather allowed her to visit the marbles shop just below the patio where he could see her.

Her mother had died of a drug overdose when Starlyn was two. No one knew how much she remembered of the frantic night of sirens, neighbors gathered on the front yard offering to take her, screaming lights.

ONE DARK AFTERNOON LAST December eight-year-old Starlyn sat on the worktable, frowning at the hanger Bobbie gave her to find the balance point. The girl had the cat's collar on a string and a seashell with a drilled hole on another. Mrs. Ashcroft—hardly more than a kid herself—said Starlyn was blossoming. Ballard Elementary. Tomas had found a studio nearby, with an apartment above. He wanted her to have stability, a chance to stay with her new friends.

She liked art and had learned her times tables from the revised poker Tomas made up. Winning hands were made of various multiples, with rules that Bobbie and Starlyn thought changed suspiciously every few days.

Starlyn slid the strings back and forth, finally finding the right place. "Look!" she shouted and Bobbie's heart stilled at the child's careless happiness. She kissed the girl, longing for the moment to last, feeling the touch of her own young self.

Now gone. On the table the upturned shell rocked slightly.

Turning solemn, Starlyn had put down the hanger and patted Bobbie's cheek. "I know," she said. "You love me."

Bobbie and Tomas had argued about the move for three horrible days.

"Get it? I don't want to be here!" he'd shouted.

"But you've made a place! You said you didn't want to uproot her again. But you're uprooting her again."

"Two years ago! She's doing great. You heard, Socialization A+."

"You don't want to be with *me*."

"Right. You're the only reason anyone ever does anything."

She turned away, unable to hide how much the blow had landed. He put his hand on the pile of velvet streamers she'd just cut. "The offer's open." A pause. "You could meet my aunt. She still rides without a saddle. She'll teach Starlyn." Another pause. "And you ..."

"On a horse?"

"That's where bareback occurs."

Big Sky—an abyss—how could she make her way in such a strange place? "They have sagebrush."

There was a moment. She could have turned. "Plus, it's such a faint offer." Say something! "We both know that." Anything.

He didn't speak.

Coward. A friend of his had started an online business—Silver City. Tomas could sell jewelry to New York, fancy tack to stables in El Paso. He could do that just as well from Ballard!

The bicycle took shape in Bobbie's hands. A bit of anger hummed through her veins, but just a little, and she felt good, productive. Someday, Tomas would be no more than a good memory.

Someone banged on the front door. Not FedEx—his knock was lighter. Not a friend; her friends worked on

Saturdays. Tomas? With Starlyn? Starting to see that Butte-was-Boring? Bobbie looked down. A glue-stained sweatshirt. Who'd put that on her? She flew into the bedroom. The maid forgot to do the wash! Where was the silk shirt she'd ironed once with every intention of going to a party? There, in a heap on the cedar chest. She looked in the mirror. Prison pale. Gloss. Hair clip. She frowned at the idiot in the mirror. Big talk—a memory. *Right*. Another bang. "Coming!"

She crossed the living room. Piles of books on the floor. Two glasses with dried orange juice by the little TV. A stack of antique kitchen utensils on the wide sill; on the floor in the corner, a moose head looking up at the ceiling. A madwoman lived here. She flung open the door.

The hefty man took a step back. "Oh," he said. "Are you OK?"

"I was just expecting..." He must be lost, or a salesman. She felt almost bent with disappointment. *Go away*. She looked at him more closely.

"Gordy?" Her husband once. She hadn't seen him in a quarter of a century. Their marriage of six months had been like a long, mostly awful date. Then he'd been tall, gangly, unforgiving. In the decades he'd shrunk and spread, his belly softly pressing against a button-down shirt, gentleman's jeans. He looked battered, just holding up.

He said, "I'll come back when..." He studied her. "You remember me," he said.

OK, the Gordy of old, a man of statements, not questions. Long ago he was on call fixing Xerox machines, but then he got into grad school in CalTech. Overjoyed, he told her they'd live in student housing, and she'd get a job at an art supplies store or someplace to support them.

"I, ah, was expecting someone else." She'd said that already. She buttoned a cuff. Instead of packing, she'd slept with one of his friends. Now she wondered, Who was that person who did such things? Gordy had cleaned out their little apartment on Capitol Hill, taking everything—the pots and pans, all her paints, her clothes, her socks. He wanted her to have nothing.

He said, "You're different."

"It's good to see you." She smiled. "I don't know why. The past. I was just thinking about the past."

He said carefully, "Me too."

They stood in the rare Seattle sun, her staked oak sapling beside them.

He said, "I've been thinking about... If...a different timeline—"

She smiled. "You've been thinking too much."

He looked up. "I know what *you're* thinking right now." He broke off a leaf.

"No, you don't. You were never good at that."

"You're thinking that I've gotten soft in my old age."

She let out a laugh. "Close enough." A pause. "Gordy, why are you here?" She should ask him in, but something in the way he planted himself across the path prevented her. His presence was a vague demand. She should be working.

He rolled the leaf, crushing it. "Truth be told, divorce number two. Just three days ago. I signed the papers and had to get out of Denver for a while. Come home to Seattle. Even though Dad's been gone for ten years."

"I'm sorry about all of that...your dad." Ten years ago. She had a sense of time collapsing. Gordy's father had done something in city government. He cooked dinners for her and Gordy. She remembered him stewing a whole chicken and serving it under a little gazebo in his house in West Seattle. His wife had died. He did the best he could. He was a big, apologetic man, and Gordy was a little ashamed of him.

Gordy said, "I miss him, you know. You don't think you will."

"*You* don't think you will."

He nodded slowly. "My mistaken ways." He gave a little smile. "I think you tried to tell me that once upon a time."

She'd met him at a party just after she graduated from Shorecrest High. She'd gotten into Parsons but New York scared her, and UW, her alternative, suddenly looked huge, full of frat boys throwing things out the windows of their broken-down Victorians. She was paralyzed. At first Gordy loved her, told her that he thought she would surprise him all his life. He took her to Snoqualmie Falls for brunch at the inn. He was awkward and charming. He told her she'd be the next John Franklin Koenig, saying *he* didn't have a creative bone in his body.

Nostalgia gripped her. She said, "Want to come in for a bit? I think I have orange juice."

She scooped up glasses and a pair of shorts on her way to the kitchen while he moved a stack of magazines off her couch but didn't sit. Behind her she could hear him walking slowly around the little room, taking note, she was sure, of the dust, the things that were broken. In a flash she remembered an argument. She'd shouted, "I create. You assess!"

"A good division of labor," he'd said calmly.

Oh, that awful calm. As they'd argued, he'd taken her forearm, held it too long; she couldn't turn her back on him. Suddenly she thought of his moods, the shake of his head when she left her hairbrush too close to his side of the sink. She'd forgotten the little things, remembering only that she'd wronged him. A thought hit. Maybe she'd blindly escaped.

She found ginger snaps that weren't too stale and her mind turned again. He was different now, wasn't he? Pleasantly worn out. Maybe she was glad to see that. In the living room she set down the tray, took the worn, leather ottoman on the other side of the table.

He sat in silence, thinking.

She took a cookie. "I've been on deadline for a project."

"Several projects," he said.

She laughed but a sense of slight foolishness came over her, a sense from her short past with him. To fill the silence, she asked if he had any kids.

He nodded. "My wife and I start mediation next week." He took a breath. "They're eight and six. The boy's eight." He sat back. "He's at soccer practice right now." His frustration filled the room. She didn't want his frustration in her room.

"And you're here," she said gently. She was always polite.

He nodded. "My wife is at the vengeance stage." He gave a slight squint of hurt or something else. His face darkened, a deep line inside one brow.

Bobbie felt a prick of alarm. Over what? He sat with shoulders slumped, his hands dangling between his knees. Lost.

She said quickly, "I have an eight-year-old niece. Starlyn. Well, really, a family friend. She's over here a lot." Maybe she would never come again.

He nodded, full of his thoughts.

He didn't ask about Starlyn, not interested. The day was slipping away.

He looked up sharply, his forehead shiny with sweat.

Another warning tick. Absurd. She said, "Starlyn is an old soul. You should hear what she says. Out of the mouths of babes and all that."

He drank half the juice, set it down. "At that age they're good at mimicking adults. When they say it, it sounds so smart but really they're parrots." He took a breath. "Cute parrots." A distracted smile.

"I just remembered that I have a meeting. Sorry." She stood up.

He stayed sitting. "Do you know that you were the one who got me through everything? Actually, I had another marriage. Number two-point-five." He ducked his head. "When I first got to Lockheed. Denver was so high and I got headaches. She taught first grade. But I kept thinking of you. You made me laugh. Maybe I didn't try. I kept thinking we could—"

"—I don't know what to say."

"Because *you* never thought of *me*." That look. Tight, focused on a mirage just over her shoulder.

She walked to the door to open it for him or run, she wasn't sure, but he was quickly at her side. He took her arm. "I shouldn't have left you like that."

"It was OK." She tried to slowly pull back but he stepped closer. She said, "We weren't meant for each other." She grabbed the door handle but he pulled her away.

"We never finished what we started," he said.

"I have to make a phone call." Where was her phone?

He wouldn't let go. He had both her upper arms. She couldn't move! She couldn't *move*.

He hissed into her face, "You were my flame. Now look at you! What flame? How could you do this?"

"What? What did I do?" The window was barely open. No one would hear her scream. Talk. Keep talking.

"You misled me," he said very quietly. "All these years."

"I wasn't even..."

He let go with one hand and yanked up her shirt. What? This wasn't happening! She twisted back and forth, but he pulled at her clothes, and her sorry breast mashed against his shirt.

"Stop!" he said.

She stopped. The world churned outside. She was erased.

He said, "That's right. This is going to happen one way or another."

Gasping for breath, she guessed, "You have a restraining order."

He shook her hard, her head flopping, but she shouted through her teeth, "I'll call the judge. You'll never see them again."

He slapped her, panting into her face, mouth wide. His breath. She could smell his ugly tongue.

"Threats." He grunted a laugh. "I'm dead. Don't you see? You took...all of you took me piece by piece." Suddenly he had his belt off. "Take and take. Nothing left." He cinched it around one of her wrists, so fast. "No flying now," he said as he yanked it, jerking her off her feet.

"You've done this before!" She bit his hand.

"Bitch." He yanked her jeans down so hard she felt skinned, turned open. His fingers pulling, probing, hurting. Her head hit the leg of the table. She thought clearly, Someone tell Starlyn, dying now, dying.

She prayed for another day. He made her kneel. She prayed for innocence. For not knowing. For childhood.

There was a sound at the door. He hesitated. She screamed. There was Tomas, his eyes wide as he lunged at Gordy. He was no match. Gordy socked him in his skinny stomach while somehow holding onto the belt, pulling Bobbie back and forth as he threw another punch. It missed. Tomas, on his knees, his stomach heaving for breath. No sound. His hair curled at his neck, the smell of his cigarettes. Bobbie pushed herself up, grabbed a meat mallet from the sill, and swung it at Gordy's head. He laughed, took it, and smashed it into Tomas's neck. There was no hope.

Except for the sirens that came close fast and stopped, and then there were two men at the door. A miracle. People moving in slow motion. A blanket around Bobbie's shoulders as a woman in a dress suit carefully took her elbow and led her to a truck. She sat in the back. Sunlight. Still falling on everything. Questions. The same questions again. She answered. Her voice answered as she watched the faces come and go. Starlyn's face in the side window of the Saturn at the curb. Bobbie lifted her hand in a wave. Was that a small horse trailer at the back? The police-woman with Starlyn got in the way. And there was Tomas in plastic handcuffs lying on the grass. Three men stood over him. The long tabs of the cuffs waved in the breeze. The men lifted Tomas up and cut off the cuffs. Someone was gently washing her face with warm water. Where did he get warm water?

Tomas and Starlyn stayed for three days. Tomas had brought the horse from the estate of a client in Woodinville. "I thought I might get you up in the saddle for a walk." The chestnut nuzzled her palm. He blew out a velvet wash of air on her injured wrist. An hour later, someone who worked for the client hitched the trailer and took him away. Something in her slipped. She would never ride that beautiful horse.

Tomas did wash, cleaned up, vacuumed. Starlyn hardly

spoke but watched both of them from the couch, read one of Bobbie's Jack London books. He worried about her.

After dinner, he and Bobbie drank coffee at the kitchen table by the window. "Know what I'm going to do?" he asked loudly enough for Starlyn to hear. The girl lifted her head.

He stubbed out a cigarette. "Get fit."

"Like weights?" Starlyn asked incredulously. He didn't even jog.

Bobbie said, "Ya, Papa, like weights?" She winced—the "papa" had slipped out. He frowned. As if they were family. Through the glass, the moon threw light against a huge flat cloud. The moment passed and Bobbie touched Tomas's arm. "You forgot—you're allergic to gyms."

He cupped her hand and smiled. "How can that be?"

She smiled back. "God only knows."

It was nearly time for them to go. Tomas went to the grocery store so Bobbie would eat when he left.

She and Starlyn sat on the front step in the damp, gray morning. The girl wore a dress, tights. The police report said that Starlyn, told to stay in the car, had grabbed Tomas's phone on the seat and immediately called 911.

"There's something I've been meaning to ask you," Bobbie said.

The girl looked up.

"That day, why did you call so fast?"

The girl shrugged, put her hands on her knees. "You screamed. It was an emergency." She was a child, cautious but not surprised that things were all right.

Nearly right. Not right. Starlyn's mother. Gordy. Bobbie's throat caught. She willed herself to be calm.

The day before, Starlyn had cried in her grandfather's

arms. Bobbie was in the bedroom, and she heard Tomas talking softly to his granddaughter. Now Bobbie put her hand on the child's back. Someday Starlyn would be alone, hurt. Shaken. Stunned with grief. Again. Bobbie said, "You saved me."

"Yup."

This girl. Rain started suddenly.

As the wind picked up, Starlyn edged closer to Bobbie on the step. Huge drops pelted the leaves of the sapling. It was a freebie from the nurseryman on top of Bobbie's order, a stick with roots. "Plant it," he said. "You never know."

"Want to know something?" Starlyn asked. She looked ahead at the wet grass.

"Yes."

"Montana isn't for me. Don't tell Da."

Bobbie could hardly talk. *Isn't for me*, exactly what Bobbie had said to Tomas, the words handed back from the center of the earth to ease the way.

A moment. The smell of grass. Bobbie said, "It's our secret."

The girl nodded.

WILD OATS

Vincent skied off the lift. He had a rising, irrational feeling. This might be the first perfect day of his 52 years. Maybe his heart would be full. He turned his cell phone to silent before zipping it into the inner pocket of his jacket. No girlfriends from years ago could call with accusations that he'd left too suddenly. Work could wait. The headlines with their distant rumble of terror could wait. Joy rose. His daughter, Elizabeth—married for the second time last month—had called yesterday and said she'd finally found happiness. His son, David, two years younger at 33, got tenure last fall in the history department of San Francisco State. Vincent had the intense sense that he'd fulfilled his obligations and was now free to do what he pleased.

Dawn had broken a half-hour earlier. The powder-covered ice field at the backside of Whistler still held a pink cast. The snow was untouched. Vincent skated in his skis up the small rise to the top of the run, pushing hard with his poles, feeling strong. He stopped. The powder sagged in waves against the lower rocks, the pink deepening to blue in the shadows. To the west, a soaring ridge of granite cupped the glacier. Vincent shut his eyes, which he did whenever he saw something beautiful, a habit since childhood. A breeze tossed ice crystals off the ridge and stung his face.

Susan, whom he'd almost forgotten, skied up beside him. He opened his eyes. She stood silently, drinking in the landscape with the same eagerness he felt, or so he imagined. She wore a black watch cap, a loose jacket, the sort of plain, rugged outfit that makes a good-looking woman even more so. She had her goggles on already, her dark hair lifting off her shoulders in the wind. So many women endlessly adjusted their bindings, their hair clips, zippers. He was glad for her company on this long weekend from California to B.C. A bright spirit, she was able to be with him without interfering.

His joy had a kind of longing to it. He'd walked out on his wife so many years ago that he could hardly remember the marriage, the daily scraping of ego against ego. Relationships had seemed more like a diversion from a quest he couldn't quite define, a need to see around some corner. He had come close to marriage several times, but each time, a heaviness had invaded his heart. The dread didn't go away until he was free. But Susan was different. She said that sometimes she went to Aspen alone, and skied for days into blissful exhaustion. He'd never before known a woman who skied alone. She wanted as much as he did to be unfettered. Free to come together, and free to leave.

"Hey there, Sweet Babe," she said with a smile. She was talking to the landscape.

He kissed her cheek, a little astonished at the clean line

of her jaw, her youth. She smelled faintly of melons, as if she'd been in someone's garden, not the ski locker in the basement room of the hotel with its aggressively clean pine odor.

She lifted her goggles with gloved hands. There was the faintest touch of violet on her eyelids. The color seemed balanced against blue shadows at the corners of her eyes. He took a breath. All this—the glacier, the wind.

He wanted to hold onto it before plunging in. He pulled the back buckle of his glove tighter. "My mother was born blind. She never saw anything like this." Vincent hardly ever told women about his mother, even when they probed for family facts. He pretended his grandmother, who raised him in a tract house in east San Jose, was his mother.

Susan took this in with the slightest lowering of her head. "She never saw you? How sad. She didn't know she had a handsome son."

He shrugged. "She died when I was a child." Her sympathy was intoxicating. He said, "Sometimes I describe things for her, mentally. Funny, I hardly remember her, but I think of her listening to me." This, he had never told anyone.

She nodded and was quiet. Perfect. "You're a good son," she said finally.

His heart soared. He rarely thought of himself as a son. Usually his slight, early memories seemed awkward, inconvenient. A moment passed. "The snow," he said.

She smiled, a brief acknowledgement of his abruptness.

A buzz over his right breast. Phone. He didn't answer. Should have turned the thing off.

Susan led the way on a line to gain speed across the snow field for a cruise from one side to the next. She skied fast, using her knees to start a turn so that she seemed to float. Vincent closed his eyes on the long stretches.

He felt like *he* was floating. The loose snow parted from the tips of his skis. He opened his eyes to take the next turn. A plume of snow rose behind Susan and caught a prism of light, throwing a rainbow in the air. Vincent whooped. Susan laughed, the throaty sound caught in the backwash of air.

They ate blueberry crepes with sour cream at the restaurant at the top of Blackcomb that was hardly bigger than a warming hut. All around them, skiers recounted how they'd caught a tip and recovered, or flown off a snowboarder's path, or made a record number of runs. Vincent felt as if he'd never been around so many happy people. It was as if death had been banished from the mountain. Why was he thinking about death?

His father left before he was born to follow a scheme of finding uranium in Bolivia, and he was five when his mother died of a tumor that invaded her brain. The fact of her existence seemed almost melodramatic to Vincent, almost irrelevant. His grandmother had shown him photographs of a tall woman with broad shoulders. In many of the pictures, she cocked her head the way blind people do, listening for sounds ricocheting from the walls. A little smile played across her cheeks.

He reached across the rough table and touched Susan's cold-flushed cheek. So smooth. "What?" she said softly. A burly, bearded man in an orange alpine jacket shoveled chili beside her.

Vincent wanted to see her quicken with his words. He said, "You ski economically. You don't waste movement."

She smiled. "I thought you were going to say something personal."

He felt caught out. He'd only given her the tip of what he felt. "I mean," he said, "this is the best day of skiing I've ever had." They'd been seeing each other for four months—whenever she was in California—but they'd never before skied together.

She smiled, then sobered. "I'm turning thirty-six today. It's a good birthday."

"You didn't tell me."

She shrugged. "I didn't want you to feel obligated. But maybe we could raise a toast tonight. Thirty-six years on this planet."

So. The day was special for her too. He should have known. Something had illuminated this morning.

Another vibration at his chest. Wi-Fi on a glacier? Ridiculous. He ignored the call. He wanted to get the moment back. Where were they? "Actually, I have a question. Not exactly personal, but ..."

"Yes?" She smiled, her hands wrapped around a giant mug of coffee.

"How come you're such a damn good divorce lawyer if you've never been divorced?" She was an attorney in a 3-woman firm in Hartford. They handled residential real estate and family law. She was the divorce specialist. Josh, his friend from Connecticut who told him about this perfect woman, said everyone wanted her on their side.

She looked at him, her smile fading. "Trick question?"

"That came out wrong. I mean, Josh says how fair and solid you are. Nobody likes divorce lawyers."

"OK."

"I'm digging myself a hole here."

"Yup."

He raised a brow. She laughed, quickly sobered. She looked at the skiers crowding into the food line. Her lips worked slightly in thought. He'd lost her. His spirits dimmed.

She said, "Certain things I never forget. One, children first. No matter what. They didn't ask for this. They don't get a vote. Custody battles need to be short and civil. I insist. My clients included." He knew she adored her nieces, five and seven, often coming from Connecticut to Mountain View to see her sister's happily pied-up family.

She gazed out the snow-mottled window, thinking.

"And rule two?"

She looked at him. "Divorces are sad but fantastic; they distill people into their basic elements, whether it's ferocity, or flexibility, or defeatedness."

"Distilled defeatedness?" he teased, though in fact he liked her seriousness.

With her fingertips, she moved her little napkin.

"Some seem destined to be hurt," she said with a half-smile. "It's what they expected all along. Men especially. You'd be surprised at how many men have that hang-dog attitude under a lot of bravado."

She looked at him. He raised his eyebrows. Her talk of hurt pierced him. In her practice, he thought, she saw people *in extremis*, losing what they'd once loved, pushing or being wrenched away from their hopes. His way was better, loving without the grinding habits of attachment that were apparently so hard to break.

"You don't expect to be hurt?" he asked her, kidding but feeling like he'd brought a pen knife to a sword dance. He wasn't accustomed, as she was, to looking at the startling flow of pain and joy behind conversations.

"Never," she said, deadpan. "I don't believe in getting hurt."

"Me either. I'm a hurt agnostic." Silly.

She rolled her eyes.

This woman. On a day he didn't expect anything.

Two kids carrying handfuls of Saltines bumped against her. "How much do you think we could get for this table?"

She unclipped her gloves. "Indeed. Onward."

HEADING BACK DOWN THE mountain, they skied lazily, in big arcs, avoiding the moguls that had begun to appear from the traffic in steeper fields. At the hotel—a 1970s replica of a 19th-century villa, called The Chateau—they showered and fell exhausted into bed. He felt excellent. He had 16 years on her, but hadn't flagged. At least at skiing.

"The nap after a day on the slopes is almost as good as sex," she said. She wore one of his T-shirts and lay propped on her back against two pillows. Her leg barely touched his under the sheet. She smiled. "Every muscle, purring."

He wanted to say something important, something to mark the well-being that swelled from his belly, his heart. He took her hand under the sheet. "Strange," he said, "but I've been thinking of my mother. I've described the whole day to her. It gives me great satisfaction." He couldn't think of a better word, one large enough to describe the expansiveness he felt.

She considered this. She didn't seem to think this talk of mothers strange. "You're lucky," she said.

His throat tightened. He thought of a boy sitting on his mother's lap. Did she touch his face? He couldn't remember.

Susan sat up a little. There was silence. Her wet hair fell on her shoulders. The melon scent was strong.

He turned and put his hand where the long bone of her thigh met her hip. He wanted her, but not yet. Right now, he wanted to feel the sheet across his arm, her smooth skin like the sight of first snow against his palm. He wanted to touch her lips with his fingertips, to part them, to part himself for her.

"I want you to be the father of my baby."

The room turned dark in the shadow of the mountain. A bulbous lamp stood on a desk by the over-large TV.

"You have good genes. You're athletic, sensitive, energetic, and you loved your mother."

Hollowness invaded his chest. Wet snowflakes appeared past the window. Had there been clouds? He threw off the sheet. "A baby?"

She lowered her chin, but spoke calmly. "My sister is so happy with her kids. Sure, they're a lot of work, but I've never seen her so fulfilled. I want that." She looked away. "I want someone who needs me no matter what. I would be good with a family. Committed."

He got out of bed. "This was just a spur-of-the-moment thing? Oh, by the way, my clock is ticking so why not be my stud fuck?"

She gave him a tremulous smile. She spread her hands on the blanket. "I've been thinking about this all day, all month."

"That's what you were thinking about?" He turned on the light. He wore shorts but felt exposed, his chest bare in the modulated heat of the hotel.

His suitcase lay open on a stand by the window. He pulled on a sweatshirt.

She said softly, "I've never seen anyone look so mortified."

He wheeled. "Why not a sperm bank?"

She snorted, touched her mouth. "They try to give you personality traits and even a video of the guy talking about his likes and dislikes, but really it's just like a shopping list—"

"—You looked into it?" He was weak with disappointment. He shut his suitcase. She'd made his hands shake, damn her.

She nodded with a little shrug.

"What I loved about you was that you were carefree."

She sat regally against the pillows. "Carefree, yes. And thirty-six." She spoke quickly. "I've liked being with you. I'd like knowing that I kissed the father of my baby and felt his breath on my face. I'd always have that."

She was thinking only about the baby.

Watching his face, she spoke even faster. "You wouldn't have to have anything to do with the baby. Or me. I could draw up the papers. No strings. I'm not asking for anything except two million sperm. I'll take it from there."

He said, "You were thinking about this the whole trip?" Not about being the first ones to lay tracks on the glacier this morning, not about the hushed feeling on the trail they'd discovered in the late afternoon, its pines quivering as they swept past.

She shrugged. He couldn't look at her. He went back to his suitcase and rummaged for jeans; pulled them on. She had no idea what children were like! Her nieces were dolls she could give back to her sister whenever she wanted. But what if those kids wanted something from *her*. He said, "Kids will eat you alive."

She took a breath. "My choice."

He turned. "I have a boy and a girl. Grown."

She closed her eyes, opened them. "I know. You told me. David and Elizabeth."

Had he? His conversations with her seemed jumbled, flashing in and out of his memory. "When they're little, they want everything. Everything! All the time." He paced the room. The snowflakes dropped past the windows like little bombs. He had to talk her out of this, not just asking him, but wanting this big, juicy *false* answer to puny mornings when the sun seems weak and for a moment, your sparse bedroom could be a hotel room, nameless, anchorless. He practically shouted, "My ex-wife took the kids to Portland. A lawyer like you worked out the schedule for visits." He wanted that to sound accusatory. "For some reason I got them around Halloween. I tried to take them places. Be a good dad. When David was five, I took them to a so-called ranch to pick pumpkins. He wanted four pumpkins, not one, and he kept screaming. He wrapped himself around a wheelbarrow that was part of a display and wouldn't let go. He was like an animal. I didn't know what to do." He sat heavily on the bed.

She got up as if she couldn't stand to be near him. "But you somehow survived," she said. She pulled on a white hotel robe so thick she seemed swathed in some kind of winter animal. She stalked to the window and looked out.

Vincent felt funny on the sheets in his clothes. Misplaced. If only she hadn't gotten up. He couldn't think. He said, "Then they grow up. And one day, they quit talking. Completely. Not even, 'Good morning, Dad.' They're not at all what you expected. I remember when Elizabeth was a teenager. Other girls wore too much makeup but she didn't wear any. She had this long braid and only one friend, a boy. As pale and silent as she was. I could never tell if he was her boyfriend or what."

He just couldn't explain how much he had wished Elizabeth would go to movies, hang out with a crowd of kids like the laughing, jostling group he often saw walking past his house. He couldn't imagine why Elizabeth didn't understand that half the battle of life was selling yourself, carving your own path. "The worst part was that without saying a word, Elizabeth was always trying to please me. She made me a tie. It had little sailboats on it. She didn't know girls didn't sew anymore. I wore it all the time, but it broke my heart. She seemed so alone."

Susan turned. "She was trying to please you because you were critical of her."

Was he? "After high school, she married that boy!"

"So she wasn't so alone."

He shouted, "Are you telling me I'm wrong about my own daughter?" He'd been reduced to shouting.

She took a step away from the window. "You *have* your story, whatever it is."

There was silence. Vincent's mind shifted. He'd been so different from his children when he was a teenager. How many times had he screamed at his grandmother to please just leave him alone? Every day, he battled her. He loved her, but took cash from her purse when she came home from her job cleaning houses in Saratoga and Los Altos. He slept through his classes so she was called into the principal's office of his middle school almost every week. When he was 14, he stole her Celica and totaled it on Pacheco Pass. At 15, he got caught using his girlfriend's mother's credit card and was sent to the juvenile facility in Santa Clara for six months.

At 18, he left his grandmother's house, taking a tiny apartment overlooking Highway 101 in East Palo Alto and working as a janitor's assistant in grubby offices of small businesses, garage door manufacturers and low-end carpet dealers on Charleston Avenue in Mountain View. As soon as he was on his own, calm descended on him. He went to night school at Foothill College and discovered that he could look at the stupid case studies in his business classes and figure out better strategies than his professors. He took a trainee job at a savings and loan and gradually worked his way up.

His children didn't even try to get away from him, or to come close. As teenagers they hardly left the house when they visited. David grew to be tall and skinny, with a huge Adam's apple. Vincent bought him hand weights; David used them as door stops. He sat in the extra room and read. Both kids were polite, agreeable. Vincent didn't quite know what to say to them. In their presence he became jolly and self-deprecating. He told them not to follow in his footsteps; he'd made a mess of his life. What did he mean by that? The strangest things slipped out in their silences. He was deeply relieved yet somehow unsettled when they grew up and their visits, now voluntary, almost stopped.

In the hotel room, Vincent tried to remember if it was his turn to speak. Susan, at the window, pulled the robe around her more tightly and yanked at the belt. "I don't usually miscalculate this badly," she said.

Her hair hung around her face. She was so different from the magnificent skier of the morning. He rose and took her hand. She didn't look at him, but at the skiers straggling back to the hotel, walking heavily in ski boots. To himself, he described exhausted people with open jackets and matted hair clomping like robots. "A baby will ruin your career," he said. "I've seen it happen, even though you think it won't." He wanted to say so much more, to sink a dagger in her heart.

She said softly, "Don't try to tell me what to do." She turned. "There's a bus at six. I'm going to be on it."

The luxury bus to Vancouver. She'd checked the

schedule. She'd been prepared for any answer. Oddly, though he'd said no, her anticipation of the no stung him.

"You're not going to ski tomorrow?" He felt foolish, unprepared, grasping. He didn't want to ski alone. The thought seemed ruinous. She'd even invaded his separate pleasures.

She shook her head and gave a little laugh. She had full, shiny lips. Her eyes were swimming. "I know you don't try to be a jerk. You can't help it. That's the part I hoped my baby wouldn't inherit." A slow blink. "Well, I guess she won't inherit it now."

He dropped her hand. "You're calling *me* names? The only thing I'm guilty of is taking you to a damn pricey place and having a good day on the slopes. Here I am just walking down the street, and you gun me down. No warning."

The bitterness in her laugh stung him. "What kind of warning could I give? You spent all day mooning about your mother. Did you ever ask me about *my* mother? Did you ever want to know what I was thinking? That talk about my work—*Dating Conversation 101*." She put her hand to her cheek. She winced in a silent cry. "I shouldn't have said that. I didn't mean mooning."

He couldn't take this all in. His sense that something could happen with Susan. She'd meant to leave him all along, whether he said yes or no. Just like that. He said, deadpan, over the crash of his heart, "You have a mother?"

She gave a little snort. Tears caught in her lashes. She said softly, with a little smile, "You bastard." She went to her suitcase on the stand in the closet. She re-folded two sweaters. He watched her. He couldn't think of anything else to do. His throat was thick. His hands felt useless at his sides.

The snowflakes whirled. He said, "What if I decided later that I wanted rights?"

She glanced up at him. "You don't want rights. That's not like you."

Stung, he said, "How can you be sure I'm so bloodless? Fatherhood can change a guy."

She turned, surprised. "It didn't change you." She took off the robe and pulled on a sweater over the T-shirt. She lifted out her hair. She was unselfconscious even though he watched her closely.

Her simple, domestic gesture unloosed something. He said, "It's true, mostly what I did for my kids was pay tuition. And now I usually don't think about them. Their existence almost surprises me. But then some mornings, usually around dawn, I'll get up and I'll need to see them. Just lay eyes on them. Be sure they're OK. I'll pick up the phone. But it will be three or four in the morning. I don't want them to think their father is crazy, so I put the phone back down."

There was a pause. "I wouldn't have pictured that."

He lifted a brow. "Me either." He smiled. A sense of defeat crept over him.

Finally, she said, "Actually I don't want to leave tonight. I'm too ragged. I could go tomorrow morning."

His heart swelled. OK. OK. He'd imagined himself alone tonight trudging through the wet snow to the Italian place on the square that he liked. To himself, he described an almost-old man, fit, unencumbered, his soft boots almost noiseless on the icy path. This man was 52 and saw 60 on the horizon. Fifty had not been so bad, but now two years had already passed.

"I was so right and so wrong," she said.

He touched her arm. "And let me at least buy you a glass of wine to make up for being a jerk."

THEY DID EAT AT the Italian place, stuffing themselves with soft bread drenched with olive oil, then Mako over spinach, laughing about how the shark had made its way over the mountains to Whistler. He gave a toast to her birthday. She said, "Except for our total incompatibility, we're the perfect pair." She put her hand on his on the white tablecloth. Her palm was soft, her fingers light.

He said, "Tell me about your mother."

She smiled. "You don't have to do this."

"I know. But I want to know about your mother." To his surprise, he did. Even if he never saw her again, he didn't want to leave empty-handed. The fire in the center of the restaurant crackled under the conversation of the guests.

Susan put her hand to her throat. "My mother was a barracuda. She handled corporate accounts in a large law firm in downtown Hartford. She made partner before women made partner. She was never wrong. She worked twelve-hour days and when she got home, she had horrendous fights with my father. He taught third grade, and she had no use for his opinion—or mine. She wanted to pick my boyfriends, my classes, even my clothes. When I was sixteen, my father left. He said he didn't want to live with someone pretending to be human. When I was in law school, she died of a heart attack. They found her slumped over her desk. I've never known if I'm more mad at her for selling my first car on a whim, or for dying before I could figure her out. She came, she conquered, she left. What am I supposed to do with that?" Finally, she paused. She looked up. "Well, that's a case of too much information."

"Do you see your father?" A strange ache rose in

Vincent's chest. Had he ever asked anyone about their father? Usually he avoided the subject.

"Yes," she said. "We've gotten very close. He retired last year. He lives in Tallahassee. When he comes to California, he takes my nieces fishing."

Fishing. With a start, Vincent wondered if his daughter would be having children soon. If she did, would her kids want to go fishing? When Vincent was young, his grandmother had taken him to a stocked pond off Highway 101 a few times, but even as a kid, Vincent had never liked the uncertainty of waiting for a fish.

Susan said, "You know, you have this habit of drifting off when you're bored. You should cover it better."

How could she say that! "I was thinking about your father."

Her voice rose. "You were not. You were thinking about some transaction or other."

"Forget it," he said. He didn't expect to be so stung.

She looked up. She bunched her napkin and put it on the table. "Why do I always end up fighting? I'm just like my mother. I feel like that's all I know how to do."

There was a pause. OK. He wanted to talk. "My mother died in summer," he said. "I don't know which month. When I'm awake at three in the morning, instead of bothering my children, I try to put myself back to sleep by thinking of my grandmother's house. Mentally, I walk through the house and describe everything. I try to get it all correct: the green chair sat next to the window, her table for bills in the back bedroom. Her bedroom, her hairbrush on its back. I catalogue everything. It makes me feel better." He paused.

Susan had her hand on the table next to her plate. She didn't move. If she'd said one thing, he would have stopped.

"The day my mother died," he said, "I climbed into my grandmother's wicker laundry basket. If I crouched, I just fit. My grandmother looked all over for me. I could hear her shouting. She went in and out of the house. She was frantic."

The crowd in the restaurant had thinned out. People going back to their hotels so they could get up for the good snow of the early morning. Susan said, "I can see your grandmother, but I can't see you."

He smoothed the front of his sweater. He could hardly catch his breath. "I don't know. Let's see. Striped shirt. Belly against my thighs. Fists on my knees." He couldn't go on.

She nodded. She put her hand on his wrist. The bill came and he put a credit card on it without looking. He said, "You don't always fight. You never fight. This was the first time."

She gave a little snort. "I vowed I'd never fight with a man again." There was silence.

He sensed a familiar shadow, like a feeling from a memory. And then he heard his son's voice. From the front desk. There was David, ducking his head at the maître d' and striding over. "Dad! I knew you'd be here."

Of any place in the world? David hugged him hard, a practice he'd taken up the last few years. Vincent tried not to say, "Oof!"

He introduced Susan. David turned back to him, "Don't look so surprised. You told me a month ago that you were coming. I've been trying to call you all day. My buddy let me use his condo, so I just came! I knew you'd have dinner here."

David had buddies?

David turned to Susan. "My Dad used to call me Mr. Spontaneous."

"Nice," she said, rolling her eyes back at him. He sat down, reached over to a newly set table and took a wine glass.

"Let me guess, Mr. Spontaneous Dad," he said. "You had the shark." He poured himself the last of the Puilly-Fuisse.

Vincent smiled, "Who are you? And what did you do with my son?"

"He grew up! It happens. And ... he just got that article accepted at JAH!"

Vincent reached back to a dim recollection of their last phone call. "The article. Great! That's right. In the *Journal of Archaic Aha's*. Stalled by the peer reviewers."

David said quietly, "Got the email yesterday. I had to tell you in person." Eyes shining.

Susan said to Vincent, "It's a history journal. JAH. The top of the field." She turned to David. "Big up, bro!" He laughed. They slapped a high five.

Vincent, puzzled, to her: "You don't read history ... do you?" All that he didn't know flying at him like space debris.

She quickly replied, "My minor at Dartmouth. I almost went that route." Back to David: "What's it about?"

Dartmouth?

David looked at Vincent when he answered. "'Stegner was Right: California's Paradise Created by Pre-Irrigation Realty Ads, Literature Review 1949-1959.'"

Pre-Irrigation? Vincent thought. He said stubbornly, "Right about what? Stegner was a novelist." Proud of his knowledge. He'd read one of his books in some required course. A jumbled plot, a longing.

"And a conservationist!" David tried to get the waiter's

attention. "For the last half of his life, he told everyone who would listen that underneath the lawns and office parks, California is a desert."

"I see." He looked at his son. The thin shoulders in a big sweater, the long fingers, one hand flat on the tablecloth. Hardly buff, but a certain weight to him now. His students would listen.

David lifted his hand to his glass. Didn't drink. "I snuck into your office and read *Angle of Repose*. Blew me away. I was 15. Been studying Stegner—and a few other things— ever since." He put the wine down. "See, Dad, it all started with you!"

Vincent took the glass and drank from it. "I don't know what to say." His eyes blurred.

Susan said quietly: "Say, 'Son, I'm so proud.'" In a louder voice: "Then order us all a massive dessert."

David turned to her. "You're reading my mind."

Vincent said, "I am." Out of sync. Meager.

"I know, Dad."

THEY ORDERED A CRÈME brûlée and a molten lava cake that the waiter set in the center of the table. Vincent's teeth ached, his spoon clattering against Susan's or David's as the two of them bantered about the colleagues David liked and the ones who were stodgy.

Stodgier than David? Vincent's quadriceps were getting tight, bewildered with sudden downtime.

Another clash over the ganache and David looked over at him, smiled. "Let me guess, Dad. Flunked 'Sharing' in first grade."

Vincent smiled back. "In all grades." His son teasing? Worlds created behind his back.

The fire crackled. David and Susan had their heads

together, chatting about ski resorts in the U.S., Averell Harriman, and the history of Sun Valley. She knew so much! The waiter disappeared to print out a new check. Vincent swallowed ice water to wash out the sweetness. An idea rose. *No. What would that mean? Mr. Spontaneous Dad. But could he? Think. Let it ride. Don't think. For once.* He blurted, "Susan and I were just talking about ... a project ..." How to explain?

Susan's mouth opened with alarm. Then a change. Surprise? Like coming around a corner and seeing a stunning glacier. A flash of ice shine. She gathered herself quickly and said with calm, "*My* project." She frowned at Vincent, warning him off.

She stopped, wiped off a fleck of chocolate on her lower lip. "My project ..." She put the napkin down.

David sat quietly. He had the ability to wait for someone else's thoughts. An in-born talent.

My genes ... improved, thought Vincent wildly. He said carefully to Susan, "Your search for one good man."

"Exactly." She stared between them, thinking.

David grinned. "O-kay." He looked from one to the other. "Is this a video game?"

Susan said, "I need a night cap. Not here. They want to close up. Where's a good place?"

"Mallard Lounge," Vincent and David replied together. Vincent heard it—the matched timbre. He laughed, giddy. Resonance in the spheres. He was part of something.

But as they swung outside, Susan took his hand, pulling him back, and said, "Didn't you say you were tired? I'll be up in a bit."

"Oh." The stars were needles. "Yes. Of course." There was the boy in the laundry basket.

In the Chateau, David headed toward the lounge, turned back. "Coming?"

"Not tonight," Vincent said. "I have to get my beauty sleep."

Susan took his son's arm.

"But I want her home by midnight!"

David laughed.

Vincent took a second shower. Midnight came and went. Of course they weren't coming back. He tried to work. The goose neck lamp on the wall by the bed didn't have the right angle. 12:30. Tick. Tick. Turned off the light. Tick. Turned it back on. Why would they come back?

He pulled on a jacket over sweats, his hair wet. He went down the wide, silent hall. Good skiers were sound asleep. He was a crazy man creeping through a castle. He should go back for shoes. Find a mission. Was he lost? The elevator appeared. That was his trouble. Lack of mission.

The bar had a warm interior like the secret world inside a chocolate egg. Vincent described it for his mother. He straightened and walked in with purpose. His grandmother had told him to do that whenever he was in trouble.

They were there! In the corner. Talking. He strode toward them. Soon, he would need something to say. David's face was flushed, his hand cupped in the crook of her elbow, a gesture of attention, as if tilting his whole body into her last point.

He looked up first. "Dad!"

"I was ... " He stopped. *Think.*

Susan touched her fingers to her throat. She said, "Your son says you told him never to donate his sperm on the first date."

His heart rose. "Yes ... exactly. A family rule. Passed

down. You know. My grandfather to my father to ... actually, I have a question. For David."

A woman at the next table looked at his feet.

He shrugged at her, turned back to David. "Do I still own that Stegner book?"

"You do. I snuck it back."

"OK, then. Carry on." He started to leave.

David brushed his jacket sleeve and smiled. "Any chance you've got a few more pages of that family manual?"

"Not a chance."

A MAN LIKE MY FATHER

y father, Coryell Hintikka, liked striding across the cherry blossom-scented UW campus in his black greatcoat. Big shoulders, dark brown, wavy hair. According to one of his eager teaching assistants, he looked like Voltaire ushering in the Enlightenment. Skinny freshmen in new slickers sometimes waved shyly at the tall, handsome sociologist featured on the cover of their Welcome Huskies packets, and the brightest graduate students caught up with him hoping to ask a question or two. They had studied his 1992 classic *The Sociology of Cities* wherein he predicted the middle class flight back to the inner cities. I wondered why *inner city* didn't refer to a giant, collective soul.

I kept this thought—and most others—from my father.

At home, he was an intellectual brute, a philanderer, a soul crusher. My mother and I kept this quiet. Almost until the very end, my mother loved walking through Seattle on her husband's arm. She was slender, pale, her hair twisted high so blond strands crossed her brow in the wet breeze.

On campus, my parents were enviously called The Couple. At home, my father shamed my mother into reading the *New York Times*, *The Atlantic*, *The Economist*, then browbeat her when she forgot senators' names or details of, say, the Superfund. Even after fighting tears through one more family dinner, she clung to the romance of the idea that my father had rescued her from an unimportant life.

She often told me that she was just nineteen when he plucked her from behind the counter of her family's block-long deli in Ballard, Seattle's Scandinavian district. Flirting with her, my father casually put his large hand over one of the hearts carved into the woodwork by the cash register and she was smitten.

Years later on a cold October evening, my parents gave an elaborate dinner party to celebrate the honor bestowed by the editors of *Sociology Today* naming my father's book one of the top five most influential works in the field in the last 50 years. My mother and I spent two weeks planning and cooking. One of my father's guests was his girlfriend Jeanne, a professor of French literature with a hawk nose, swinging hair, and an acid tongue. A black-haired Milady de Winter. For the first time, he had brought the enemy into our fortress, a Victorian on the north side of Capitol Hill that my mother had reshaped through the years. Milady's undeniable presence was against my parents' unspoken agreement.

While my mother served meatballs simmered in milk with a flat potato bread called lefse, my father, sitting at the head of the long table next to me, reached under the tablecloth and patted Milady's thigh. My mother, standing by the sideboard, froze, squeezed her eyes shut.

Father was knowingly, cunningly challenging her

existence. I think he just wanted to see how far he could push her.

Strangely, in those days I thought of my cerebral father as a farmer on a tractor with a huge windshield (did tractors have windshields?). My mother and I—and actually his girlfriends and students, too—were the gnats that happened to strike the glass. Occasionally he would deliberately veer into one of us, but usually he had his sights on a distant horizon, a darkly setting sun that impulsed him forward as he cut long rows into the earth.

My mother jumped off the Aurora Bridge the morning after the book party. In mid-air, she must have had a wonderful view of the hills of her old neighborhood.

For weeks after the funeral, my cheeks ached and I couldn't speak, my eyes turned cold, my ears were packed with cotton. I was seventeen.

My father dramatically played the haunted genius who had been all too human and now was sorry, sorry, sorry. His friends—a group of men from the statistics and history departments who joined the faculty about the same time he did—came to our house and sat with him. I put the casseroles their wives made in our huge old refrigerator. My father wearing socks and a sweatshirt with baggy corduroys put his head in his hands at the long table and told his friends that he took full responsibility. I lingered in the kitchen and listened. He seemed to have sponged up my mother's death and left none for me.

To demonstrate his profound sense of guilt, my father dumped Jeanne (and quietly enlisted an admiring columnist for the *Seattle Times* as his temporary new lover). He took on a huge teaching load, many more classes than any full professor in the history of the sociology department. His friends told him how brave he was.

Two months after my mother's death, I cooked his morning egg too hard. He held onto the plate and sent it flying into the sink saying it tasted like a poached baseball and that I cooked like I thought, carelessly and with no finesse.

My jaws ached and I wasn't sure if this was a day I could make sense. "Leave me alone. I'm mourning my mother," I said.

He wore the rumpled plaid shirt and red tie he would teach in. "All the more reason to pay attention. You don't want to go down in sloppiness."

"Go down where?" I asked. "Give specifics." His line. Did he think I was my mother? She'd cry. Not me. I had dreamed the night before that someone dropped me from a great height and my head cracked open on the sidewalk. In the dream, I sat up and thought calmly, *I wonder if I'm dead?* If my mother had miraculously hit land, would she have broken something but still breathed?

My father snorted. There was a pause. He put the empty plate on the table, looked at it. He said gently, "Go down to hell, little girl." He glanced up at me. "She was the love of my life," he said. "So I had to damage her." He rubbed the corner of his mouth with one finger. "I knew it at the time. I just couldn't stop." His face was damp. With tears?

"You could've stopped," I said. She was gone.

"I could have." He cried. I let him fold me against his chest for a minute. Then he went to class.

I stood in the kitchen numbed by the kitchen towels folded on the counter by the sink, by the salt and pepper shakers shaped like bluebirds that my father disdained as kitsch, by the clean coffee spoons up-ended in a red glass the way my mother's Norwegian family always did. I turned to break the hold of the kitchen.

YOU WOULD THINK THIS conversation with my father might have softened things between us, but within days he seemed to forget it ever occurred. If anything, he became even more inexplicably furious. He criticized the black outfits I wore to Roosevelt Public High School as "trite weeds," asked me why I let my mother's house get so dirty, and started pawing through my backpack to find graded papers—I wrote like a zombie, but the grades were usually good. In the margins he scrawled "fatuous" or "you've got to be kidding me." I began staying out late with my boyfriend An Song, who avoided my father. My father couldn't bear to be avoided. Once, at midnight, he locked me out. My house keys were mysteriously gone from my backpack. I jimmied the bathroom window and slid in over the radiator. My father told me the next morning that I needed to understand the consequences of sneaking around and wasting my potential. His own sneaking was apparently beside the point.

Finally, early one September night, I came home to a dark house. My father seemed gone and I couldn't get in. He knew I was taking my SAT test for college the next morning. Was he inside with his old girlfriend Milady? Was he deliberately ruining my future? Rain battered the porch overhang. Did some ancient gripe he had against the universe well up, making him want to defeat someone, me, just because he could?

At the time, I didn't wonder about his motives or think about anything. I pounded on the front door of our porch. No answer. I went to the side door at the kitchen. The bathroom window. All locked. How could he? I screamed so the neighbors could hear, "Open up! I'm your *daughter*, you bastard!" Nothing.

I took the little path back to the street and walked for an hour in the rain to An's room above the Pike Place Market. An was 28, a ceramicist who lived in Seattle during summers and some winter weekends. A gallery in the Post Alley showed his bulbous vases and huge plates in strong, layered colors—chartreuse and shades of violet. When not in Seattle, An lived in Santa Barbara where he made new work. My father knew none of this.

I asked An if I could go home with him to California on the coastal train on Monday. He leaned on the overpainted door jamb, his shiny hair that I loved brushing his shoulder. "Yes," he said, kissing me on the forehead. He held me away and looked in my face. "You're freezing." That wasn't why I could hardly feel his lips. "Let me run the water hot in the shower."

I lived in An's large, second-story apartment near the beach and got a job at Trondheim Sandwich and Pastries. The work suited me. I liked slicing off chunks of liverwurst and labeling the wooden markers naming the cheeses. I loved the smell of buttery sandbakkel tarts and rolled krumkake. I figured I was trying to inhabit my mother's life, re-animate her. Why not? That seemed like a good place to start.

In the evenings, An taught me to draw. Later, as he slept, I arranged kelp bulbs and twisted pieces of driftwood on the kitchen table and tried to capture the bulk and weight of them. An and I had a good arrangement, nothing more, nothing less. I treasured being able to slide down beside him in bed at 3 A.M. and have him turn drowsily to say, "I have to check the kiln in an hour. What could we do between now and then?"

When he left each summer, I fed his tortoise shell cat,

and sketched the two square, cluttered rooms of our apartment a thousand times. Then another thousand. I graduated to moving objects and sat very quietly on the beach in my baseball cap trying to catch the line of a volleyball player's arm or the twist of his shoulder. After a while, the regulars ignored me.

That September, An flew home to his family in Hong Kong for three weeks. He'd told me frankly that he was going to see a woman called Ling whom he'd known since he was five years old. He came back alone, but we'd lived together for six years and I could see that he'd changed. We bought him a cot for the far corner of the main room. One night, late, we sat on the cot in the dark. "I can't do this," I said. "I miss you too much." I turned to him. "No one would know."

He shook his head as he cried, his shoulders bent. From the side chair, the cat lifted his head as I rose and went to bed.

With this new arrangement, another year passed. I lied about my education and got a part-time position teaching adults beginning drawing Tuesday and Thursday evenings at the downtown rec center. By the time I turned 25, I was almost happy.

That October An flew home to his family in Hong Kong and married Ling. We arranged for me to keep the apartment. At 4 one morning, I wrote to him: "I now understand the phrase, 'I'm happy for you.' You saved my life. You deserve heaven on earth. Please send my warmest regards to Ling. She must have done something right to get you." I put down my pen that had a flat nib I sometimes used to give a sketch a filled line. Zeus lay down on my feet. During the day he was a hellion, but now he didn't even purr, as if that would disturb me. The only movement was of his soft belly rhythmically pressing against my toes as he breathed.

THREE DAYS LATER, I came home to a message on the phone from my father. I had never given him my cell phone number. I only spoke to him every several years, usually on New Year's Day when he called as if to take inventory of exactly where his genes were. Most days, I could barely imagine that he was my father.

The message said that he was dying. He was reduced to *this* to rope me back into his life! Rage rose so quickly I had to steady myself against the battered wood table that still smelled slightly of rotten sea things. My father's resonant voice that could hold 200 undergraduates in thrall had roughened a little. A faint rasp darkened the ends of some words. He said he had a proposition for me. He wanted to discuss it in person. Was there any way I could fly to Seattle this weekend?

Of course not. Was he crazy? I snapped the phone line off the jack, took the phone down the fire escape and tossed it in the heavy, scratched Dumpster. Damn him. Dying of *what*, pray tell?

He answered my cell phone on the tenth ring. "Dying of what?" I demanded.

"Emphysema."

"You don't smoke."

"Other people did."

"What about a transplant?"

"Enlarged heart. Congestive. If I don't suffocate, I'll probably die of a big heart."

"Jesus. The irony."

Dryly, "Well said."

"Please don't comment on my comments. It's so post

modern." I was scared, my voice high pitched, silly. I still sounded ridiculous when I talked to my father.

I STOOD ON CAPITOL Way and looked up at my childhood home, which was on a slight, grassy rise with a hedge of gangly rhododendron. Painting taught me to start in the back, with air. Santa Barbara air can be almost as misty as Seattle's, but light bounces through it from low, pink and yellow adobe buildings, from dew on front yards filled with ice plant, from the sand that threatens to overtake any vacant spot. How it glistened. The air in Seattle, especially in the fall, is overloaded with the darkness of green things reaching for the sky. Thick grass along the walk to the porch seemed to spill chlorophyll into the almost-black leaves of the rhododendron against the heavy, black-streaked bark of our neighbor's cypress. The mist thickened above our stone chimney into freighted, unmoving clouds. The sun did not exist.

Yet I was almost faint with longing. My mother had discovered this house when she was a young bride, as she put it. Built in 1904, the house with steeply-pitched roof was an abandoned derelict with floors so rotted that when she took my father to see it, a floorboard in the living room gave way under his foot. My mother replaced, sanded and stained or re-painted almost every surface in the house. It was her refuge and mine. It was the reason I believed that objects have a life worth drawing. Even when the brain goes quiet with grief, the narrow back stairs lighted by three scalloped fixtures live on.

My father held court with his students in the galley kitchen, sitting on the linoleum counter, his feet on the seat of a chair while he argued and laughed with them. My mother and I climbed the stairs behind the kitchen to her "office" in the attic. She paneled it in mahogany siding she found at a demolition sale in Fremont and furnished it with large wicker chairs from the same sale. We called it our sun room.

I could see the sun room window next to the slate chimney. The only way to get inside would be to alert my father that I was there, then get past him. Maybe pick him up and throw him off the porch. My nervous jokes made me more tense. I climbed the three porch steps to the door. It had a small inset of stained glass at eye level. I could see my father in miniature next to his rows of books. I gave one sharp knock. He jumped a little, then slowly took off his glasses and came to the door.

He looked like someone had gone inside him and extracted about a third of his stuffing. His broad shoulders were racks of bone and the folds around his eyes drooped to skin puddles in hollows beneath his pupils. The porch held the humid intimacy of a tent in the rain, but I stood back in confusion. I hated confusion. I hated him. Then why was I so glad to see that old plaid shirt of his and the big, slow smile. I imagined how I looked, my feet planted apart, the wavy hair I got from him, blowing wildly in the gusts that slid down the trees like invisible waterfalls, the creases of my eyes, my mother's blue eyes.

He glanced out to the curtain of rain sliding off the eaves, then back to me, the tiniest hesitation. My father hadn't been a man to hesitate. Finally he reached out his large hand and shook mine. I went to kiss him and he stepped back.

I laughed nervously. "OK." Not OK. His palm was papery, as if newly, delicately constructed.

We sat in the living room with five narrow windows. A fire blazed behind the black wrought-iron curls of the screen. My father didn't offer me food or drink, but launched right in. "The doctors say I have about a year," he said, "and I want you to live with me for that time and pretend to be my daughter."

"Nice. Sarcasm," I said. "Don't feel sorry for yourself. It's unbecoming."

He merely nodded, no retort. Since I'd seen him last, freckles had appeared at the top of his forehead as if someone had sanded him down to a new layer. He touched the freckles with long fingertips. "There would be no nursing, cooking, or cleaning. I have plenty of help. I'm rich, you know." He looked up.

"Me, too," I said. That sounded hysterical.

"I just want you to keep me company. And to be honest, to let my friends know that you didn't desert me completely."

My throat hurt. My feet in wet sandals ached as if I'd walked miles though the Lyft driver had dropped me right at the curb. My father winced as if a little tremor ran through his body. Wrinkles darted across his cheeks. Was he in pain? Wanting me to think he was in pain? I said, "You could have told them I was dead or in Argentina."

"You're still a ten-year-old."

"It was horrible. Robbery on the pampas! My steed and I almost escaped, but then argh! Death by Bolas."

My father gave a little shake of the head as if shaking me off. Such a familiar gesture. He rarely wanted to be disturbed by what someone else said. He spoke, the cords of his neck shivering. "If you last the year, you get the house. Otherwise, I'll give it to the U."

The fire crackled and a log fell. "Deal?"

"This house?" I couldn't hide my astonishment.

He shrugged with one shoulder and smiled, "You're the daughter. It's natural."

"I always thought it would go to the girlfriend of the hour. Whoever lands on the chair when the music stops, they get the prize."

"They teach you crudeness in Santa Barbara?"

"No, I taught myself, thank you." My mother's house. The lovely bead board under the chair rail in the dining room. The long rooms with high ceilings that I'd painted standing on the top step of a giant ladder. The leaded windows with wavy glass in diamond panes. My bedroom by the back of the house looking out on the pear tree. My young self returned to me. The attic.

I said, "Let me breathe for a minute." I crossed my legs. The broad arms of the flowered chair were clean, the room tidy, my father's magazines piled in the leather holder, the deep window sills free of dust. My father was telling the truth about his help. "There must be a catch." I couldn't help myself.

"No catch. I've been de-fanged, as you can see."

My mother and I had spent a whole day hand-rubbing walnut stain into the wide planks of the floor at my feet. The next day, we put on the lightest coat of vurethane we could mix to keep it matte, not shiny. It still looked good, maybe a little darker. "One rule," I said. "You have to let me sketch your friends. I'll sit in the corner and they'll forget about me."

He compressed his lips in a half-smile. "You're still drawing?"

I nodded, bracing myself.

"People?"

I nodded again.

"Narrative art. Didn't they tell you the center isn't holding?"

I hissed, "Unlike you, I believe that there's something outside myself that's interesting. What's more interesting than the figure? An infinite number of positions. I believe the line I make has something to do with the position of the figure, the person. At least *something*." My emphasis sounded defensive. I thought, Never defend, never apologize. That had been my rule with my father since I was a teenager. What had happened to me? I'd gotten soft. I thought of the gentle way An looked studiously to the side when I spoke, always waiting until I had finished my entire thought. Then asking me more about it.

My father snorted in amusement, started to speak.

"—second rule," I cut him off. "No criticisms. None. Nada."

The amusement shifted. He put his hand on his knee, a large, over-turned bowl of bones. "I'll burst." The spreading smile.

"And no Jeanne."

The smile stopped. He lifted his palms. "Of course not."

I LOVED RULES. AN taught me three about drawing:

1. Draw what the figure is doing not what he looks like. This pertains to all figures, especially models who are not moving.

2. Never draw your way out of trouble. Instead, design your way out of trouble. This pertains to all subjects, especially those in nature. To understand this, look at Rembrandt's drawings.

3. Feet are notoriously hard to draw, unless you're Rembrandt. If you get in trouble with feet, lay a shadow across them. This will, strangely, anchor your figure.

I moved into my father's house, that is, my house. I tried to get one good, complete drawing of his helpers before he dismissed them. He fired the little, strong respiration therapist with the knot of hair at her nape because he couldn't stand the color of her nail polish (too orange).

At lunch one rainy day two months after I moved in, he barked at the cook/housekeeper with the jutting cheekbones that if he'd wanted a metallic taste in his chicken salad (she'd put in curry), he would have asked for it. He told her to go home and not come back. She glared at *me* and left.

My father, panting, went into the front room to wait for the new respiration therapist. I stayed in my mother's kitchen. I didn't want to talk to him. I had thought our agreement about criticism covered everyone in the house, but of course it didn't. I thought of the housekeeper's withering whisper to me as she gathered her bag, "I wouldn't let my *children* act like that." I was implicated—I'd accidentally touched my father's web. Our plates and glasses sat on the kitchen table all afternoon. The spoons in the glass seemed to scoop grayness. Rain scattered against the window over the sink at random intervals, as if someone were spraying a hose at us.

I missed the patch of weedy sand that led from my apartment (now sub-leased) to the beach. I missed An. I missed my walk to work at the deli barefoot across the beach, my shoes in my hand.

I'd bought my mother's brand of dish soap and its faint orange smell rose from the linoleum counter. The smell of despair. I sketched my father's coffee mug over and over. It became lumpy and bled into the darkening back of the chair. His unused spoon lay like a weapon at an angle. The slight wrinkle in the heavy tablecloth was a bunker.

My father stalked in. It was 3 PM but almost as dark as night outside. He said, "You could at least pick up a dish."

"Not in my job description." A pause. "And I don't want to become my mother."

He sat in his chair with an elaborate sigh. I closed the notebook. He picked up the spoon and I felt like he destroyed a landscape I was just figuring out. He glanced at the book and said, "You blame me for your lack of success."

I closed my eyes. "I don't want to split hairs with you over what constitutes a criticism." I *was* successful. Almost. If only I had my G.E.D., and someone to pour out my heart to besides my e-mails to An, and a venue to show my work besides one tiny gallery in downtown Santa Barbara and the dark wood walls of the deli. I felt myself sag, my shoulders tilting forward, my stomach caving—the posture of my youth. Damn him to hell.

He raised a brow and leaned back in the chair. I couldn't tell if he knew he hit the mark. Before his afternoon therapy, his face paled and now his lips were mottled with gray. "I should have been a better father." He half-closed his eyes in self pity.

I said fiercely, "Start now."

He looked at me. "I was hoping you would come to the living room to sit with me and chat. I waited for you."

"You don't *chat*."

He gave a little smile. "I was lonely. Am lonely."

"You just got rid of a perfectly good housekeeper. She was a great conversationalist."

A pause. He looked at me and I wondered if he saw my

mother's thin lips, her long neck. At last, he said, "Did I tell you that my father taught me to read?"

I knew that his father Anton had lived in Olympia and been in charge of Special Collections at the main city library. My father's mother ran off with a state senator and Anton died of a massive heart attack before I was born. My mother had remarked once that her father-in-law was a miserable human being who felt the world never appreciated him. He was tall, very thin, ate almost nothing (a sin in her book), and was as terse as my father was talkative.

Needing something to do with my hands. I got up to make coffee. My father couldn't drink his beloved Stoli shots any more, but he still downed gallons of coffee, the one taste we shared. I wondered if his gloomy father drank coffee or was a health nut. I said, "You never talked much about Anton."

My father said quickly, as if he might run out of breath, "When I made too many mistakes on the words, he'd take a book in each hand and box my ears. I still have a ringing in them." A pause. A little smile. "Maybe that's why I was never good at listening."

His father hit him? The room stilled. I stopped pouring beans into the grinder. "How old were you?"

"Four."

Tenderness crept over me. I didn't want to be tender, but the words came out, "You must have been terrified."

He shrugged. "My father said that at the rate I was going I was never going to live up to my potential."

"You were a little boy." I had thought that my survival depended on never forgiving. My mother's error had been to forgive too quickly. When she couldn't do that anymore, she didn't know how to live.

My father touched his chin with his first two fingers.

They were bent a little at the last joint. His chest had a very slight list to the right, as if the agony of trying to get enough oxygen had distorted him. The last hour before his therapy was the hardest.

I sat in my chair. The beans made a comforting racket as I touched the cuff of my father's shirt . "You never told me."

Again, no hesitation, as if he had planned this. He nodded. "The awful thing is that I'm a lot like him." A breath through flared nostrils. "I'm drawn to weakness." A quick glance at me and then back at the table. "I can't help it. My students. A weak argument and I have to smash it. They called it brilliance." Another glance. "Fools."

I said softly, "You tried to destroy *me*."

Quickly, like a confession. "I was jealous of your youth."

"My mother had just died."

He pushed out several breaths. The therapist was late. My father could die right there with my hand reaching over to pat his cheek, to push away his tears. How did we get to this? He said in a whisper, "You could go on. I couldn't."

"I couldn't go on! I was scared." I rose and kissed the side of his bent head. The thick waves of his hair smelled dusty.

"You could. You did. Look what you've become."

FOR THE NEXT THREE months, I lived in the attic of our house, making the broad wicker sofa into my bed. My father's night nurse, a burly retired paramedic, took my old bedroom. During the day, I sketched my father's friends and former students as they arrived in twos and threes for Saturday lunch or for dinner or just drinks by the fire. When I asked my father for more stories, he shrugged and said, "I've already played on your sympathies enough."

I made him coffee because the housekeepers could never get it right, and I brought him and his guests smoked salmon and capers with crackers I made like my mother because they had the right texture of crispness and just the faintest chew in the middle.

Occasionally my father caught my hand before I put down the square cushion on the corner bench by the last of the five living room windows. I'd smile at him and take out my working notebook to become a silent mouse in the corner.

One of the grad students said in passing that he'd heard Professor Anouih just won the PEN translation prize. I kept my hand moving blindly over the page. Milady. The gangling student rocked slightly on the ottoman, rambling a little. "A Moroccan poet. I don't know her work. Guess I'll have to look it up. Is Jeanne still at Simon Frazier?" Grad students enjoyed using first names.

My father nodded, his gaze squarely on the student. "She's from Vancouver," he said. Silence except for the crackle of the fire. I got up and made a fresh pot of coffee and the smell seemed to enrich the whole house.

My father's most frequent visitor was Travis Anderson, the statistician who had "done the numbers," as he said, for the famous Holmes study showing that even good events in one's life, like a happy wedding, create trauma so deep that one is more likely to, say, get in a car accident soon thereafter. In other words, if you're very happy or very sad, watch out. I was watching out. I was trying to believe in my father. I drew him as he sat wheezing by the fire with his old friend. One March night, their talk dwindled as wind blew like crashing waves through the cypress. My father's knees were splayed, his feet in socks flat on the wood floor. Without weight on them, his feet weren't very interesting. Yes, they were, I just couldn't get them right. The metatarsal jutted without relation to muscles or sinew. I couldn't reveal the architecture of the foot under the knit of the sock. Frustrated, I laid on shadow. It didn't do the anchoring it should. Oh well. I moved over the page to Travis's long frame as he rubbed his knees and gazed into the fire. I drew the bend of his frame. Wrong. I laid a line next to the first. Almost. Again. Now, several Travis's sat in the old leather chair.

I looked at the man. Was he thinking about my father's coming death? Back to the drawing. In my hands, the bones of Travis's face got longer and longer with each stroke and his spine curved down unnaturally but with finality into the chair. I was not unhappy with the way the stray early lines made his figure possess the chair and not. If only I didn't have that damned, awkward shadow of my father in the other corner.

Travis got up. I couldn't remember if he and my father had been talking. Travis said, "OK, I'll see you tomorrow."

My father nodded. Lately, he'd been holding his chin out over his chest like a turtle. Sometimes at night, he coughed for long minutes, and I heard the night nurse cooing to him. He looked up. "It'll be fun," he said to his friend.

Travis left with a clattering of his umbrella and coat and mumbles of thanks to me (for what?). I came over to adjust the fire. Kneeling, I poked at embers, ash.

"What will be fun?" I asked my father.

There was a long pause. I thought he might be asleep. He'd laid his head off to the side on the pillow I'd propped up. "A little dinner party," he said. Wendy is fixing everything." Wendy, the new cook hired on Sunday to replace the one my father said treated salt like an entrée. He rubbed his cheek along the pillow, an odd gesture of pain? of feeling the comfort of the cushion? of pleasure in just being with me? Hope rose. Fuck hope.

"Are you all right?" I asked him. The wind had died to a pleasant rustle. A sense of near peace spread through me.

He wheezed, rolled his eyes. "Perfect."

I turned, smiled. The heat scorched my knees and the side of my face but I didn't mind. I wanted this evening to last. "Travis is happy to be here."

Another smile. "I'm happy to be here."

That faint self pity, but what did it matter? Tomorrow I'd try again to draw my father. For now, I had the floor-boards warmed by the fire under my bare feet, the folds of the linen curtains my mother and I had made, my father's unhurried willingness to just sit without reading or arguing. "Me, too," I said.

I GOT UP EARLY the next morning, drove my father's Buick and bought bunches of iris, jonquils, and sunflowers (in March? Forced from a hothouse in eastern Washington?). I propped the flowers wrapped in foil and newspaper on chairs at my table on the third floor of Howell's Café by the big windows. I drank my small carafe of coffee called a hottle. Ferries forged lanes across Elliott Bay. The sun crawled up over the fog bank and laid stars across the water.

An's fourth rule was that if you don't start a drawing right, it'll never be right. I wasn't so sure. Maybe anything could be salvaged.

WENDY HAD EIGHT CHILDREN, all grown. She toasted almonds for the halibut I'd gotten at the market, washed collard greens for sautéing, and made buttermilk biscuits. I was glad the meal would be little like what my mother would make. I arranged flowers and set them in large vases in the living room, dining room, and even kitchen. Working beside Wendy, I stirred together a mango salsa and also a hoisin sauce that An had shown me. Wendy, pushing at the side of her very short hair, laughed and said that she'd resisted fusion until now. I plugged my iPod into my Father's CD player and turned up the volume on some twangy country songs. Wendy, laughing, gave an exaggerated drawl, "You white folks sure do like some stupid rhymes." I grabbed her hand and we danced in the little kitchen. Something was happening to me.

My father came out of the back bedroom. "I thought I told you," he deadpanned to Wendy, "no frivolity in my house."

She mirrored his stare and upped her Nashville drawl, "Believe me, Dr. Hintikka, this ain't no frivolity. This ain't hardly music."

He grinned. Unbelievable. Had I forgotten my father's non-ironic smile? A dimple appeared among the scattering wrinkles and his eyes glistened. That smile, like a steelhead breaking the surface, gleaming. Anything was possible. I said to my father, "Watch out, or I might dance with you."

He took my arm and waltzed me in the little space between counter and chairs. He dipped his head with the beat like a little boy trying not to make a mistake in the rhythm. He reached up to let me twirl. Rhododendron blossoms waved outside the window. I bumped against Wendy's broad backside. "I want hazard pay!" she cried.

The guests started arriving at 7. There were 19 of them and they admired the flowers and talked about the weakened dollar against the euro and told stories of their travels to Hanoi, the Antarctica, and Santa Fe. I sat at my chair at the corner of the long table. Earlier, Wendy had found silver candlesticks, cleaned off the tarnish with almost-dried polish she found in the back of the cupboard, and lit white candles. On the buffet she put five votives. "This isn't going to look séance-ey, is it?" I'd worried.

"No," she said without turning, "it's going to look Four Seasons-ey. We're going to make this poor old house glow!"

It did. The guests I remembered as acerbic and competitive settled into quiet chatter. Someone told an ancient golf joke and everyone groaned good-naturedly. There was a knock at the door.

I jumped up, looking forward to seeing another person from my father's past, my past.

It was Milady. With a little girl who was trying to tug away. The street behind them had become a river of rain. Milady had aged into a tiny, brittle stick of a woman with flat black hair and lines shooting around her bright mouth. No.

That sly mouth. She said, "Oh, you're home. I didn't expect you home. I've brought my daughter, she needs to meet ..."

I shut the door.

I stalked back into the radiant dining room, my heart shrunken to a ball of spit.

Guests saw my face and stopped talking. I said loudly to my father, "Jeanne will not be joining us tonight. Nor will her daughter. Possibly yours. Just one stray daughter to add to the pile. But you will not get to watch this one politely squirm. So sorry. That would have been fun. Your last hurrah. You win. I'm done." I turned to the women with big necklaces they'd bought for a song in desperate countries and the men who smelled of old wool and ant-acids, "He's all yours. Let's hope he didn't poison your dinner."

I walked through the kitchen and up the stairs. The fixtures were bloodless moons. I'd piled my sweaters and jeans on the glass table. I threw them in my duffel. I couldn't see. I fumbled for my cell phone in a jeans pocket and tried to work the Uber app. It went blank. I called Yellow Cab but got a steakhouse. Why was a waitress answering a taxicab phone? She told me to try again and I muttered an obscenity at her for not being a cabdriver and she slammed the phone. So I tried again and miraculously got a dispatcher.

My father, panting heavily, ducked under the slanting beams of the ceiling, and stood with his chin cantilevered over his withered neck, "I didn't ask her to come. It was a coincidence." His breath rattled in his throat. The skin around his eyes quivered. "You said she had a baby with her?"

"Don't even," I said. "Just die. Get it over with."

"Honestly." He held onto the raw 4 X 4 in the middle of the tiny room. "I haven't seen her in years. Travis must have told her about the party." A breath. "There was a baby?"

I crushed a sweatshirt into a corner of the bag. I could send for the bigger things later—Wendy would pack them for me. "Not a baby. Six. Seven. Talk about careless," I said quietly. "For once, just—"

"—I have everything to lose here. Why would I ask her … do that? To you? To me? I love you."

I turned. "Heaven help me." My mind roared yet a tiny doubt sneaked through. Milady *had* looked surprised to see me. She loved drama, but coming to a party to claim my father had … That was too far, even for her. My mind whirled. My mother had hated drama. I hated drama.

My father sat heavily in the broad chair. "And you love me." His wheezing was wind in weeds.

I resisted his wheezing, the sheen of his face that could have been sweat, could have been tears. "I try not to," I said quietly.

"If you didn't, you wouldn't have such a big chip on your shoulder."

I sat on the rumpled quilt on the sofa, shook my head. Shook it again. My spirits slowed. The tip of the cypress was a dark shape outside the window. I knew my sharpness chased people away. Sometimes I lay in my bed in Santa Barbara and listened to the college kids on the street below laughing and sometimes whooping, and I'd think I was from another planet. I looked at my father. He blinked fast. He gasped for air. I was trapped in his meanness, mine. I was alone. The wind whispered through the shingles. I said, "You're right. But you get a black mark for criticism."

He finally managed a big breath. "When I was ten—"

"—you were never ten." I would always be alone. "I don't care if your father beat you to a pulp. I can't live like this."

A second big breath. He was reviving from the long climb up the stairs. "He did beat me to a pulp. He had big hands like mine."

"I'm not listening."

"He used various excuses. The worst time, I'd spilled a drop of ginger ale on a copy of *Moby Dick* in his collection from the estate of the John Vancouver family. I was reading it when I wasn't supposed to. He pushed me into the bathroom and hit me so hard he broke my clavicle."

I squinted against the light spreading from the hanging

lamp my mother had suspended from the low rafters. "Which page," I said, exhausted.

"Pip falls overboard. 'And Pip saw God's foot upon the treadle of the loom, and he spoke it, and therefore his shipmates called him mad.'"

The hard wicker back of the sofa against my neck seemed unyielding.

He said quietly, "I never hit you."

"So that was the standard?" Sarcasm was my instinct.

He shrugged and said sadly, "Maybe so."

I nodded. I wasn't sure what I was agreeing to. Someone rang the bell. My father and I both gave a start. The taxi. Or Milady trying again. We looked at each other. Three more rings. Then the sound of a car backing into the street and leaving. I didn't go to look. "OK," I said. I would decide later what was OK and what wasn't.

I could hear the party breaking up below. The front door opening. More car engines being started. My father nodded. "OK," he said. Maybe he was deciding, too.

FOR THREE MORE MONTHS, we lived in the same house and were civil to each other. I knew I would one day track down Milady and get the real story, but for now, I drew sketches of Wendy and gave most of them to her. She said she was going to sell them for big bucks someday.

My father got sicker. Most of the time he stayed in bed with oxygen hooked up. When I sometimes met him in the kitchen, his cheeks were dented from the tubing. When he sat down, I'd kiss him on the forehead. When Wendy had to take one of her grandkids to the dentist or otherwise babysit, I poached his eggs and made him toast with orange marmalade, his favorite. Why not? He was my father. I couldn't figure out anything else.

One clear day in June as Mount Rainier presided over the city, I went to the mailbox and found a letter to my father from the Development Office of the University of Washington. I didn't usually pry into his mail, but suspicion overwhelmed me and I opened it. "Dear Dr. Hintikka: In appreciation for your generous gift, we would like to invite you to the … ."

I ran up the three stairs of the porch and into the house. My father was slumped in his chair by the fire, a closed book on his lap, the book I'd fetched for him from the new, downtown library. I held out the letter and said evenly, "You already gave away the house."

He looked up. Folds of skin tented his eyes. He gave a short sigh, almost a snort. "I did."

"All right," I said, turning. "The end. Finally."

He became very agitated. He put his palms to his temples. "How do you think I could afford all this care?" He looked at me, a twist of a twisted body. I towered over him.

He cried, "I couldn't go to a hospital! I couldn't live under the rules of some grandiose intern. You know I couldn't. It would have killed me."

"No jokes. We're past jokes. You gave away the house before I got here."

"I had to stay in the house. And I had to have you. This is my life. What's left of it. I love you."

"You're a monster."

"I love you. You have to believe that."

"I don't."

ALL WAS LOST, SO I could do whatever I wanted. What did I want? For some reason, I stayed in the house. The nurse said my father wanted strawberries so I got some at the market and cut them into tiny pieces so he could eat them.

I covered them in cream the way he liked. I don't know why I did this. The nurse said he loved them.

Mornings, I found the *Times*, usually under the cypress tree, and laid it on the kitchen table for him. I put a single lily in a vase for his tray. My mind was dead. I didn't know what I was doing.

He died two weeks later about midnight. The nurse called the ambulance and then knocked on my door. I didn't go to see him. I'd seen enough of him. The nurse went with my father's body.

I wandered the house. I had the sensation that my mother had died again. I washed the kitchen counters. I put a fresh tablecloth on the long table. The cloth billowed and sank. I went into my father's room. The nurse had hung his coat on one side of the high-backed chair by the little bedroom desk. I stared at it for a long time. It was a thick wool with wide lapels. The black had softened to charcoal and the lower hem brushed the floor.

The medical equipment stood in a corner on a metal table that must have belonged to the agency supplying the nurse. Should I call someone to get it? I couldn't move.

Finally, my legs ached too much to stand. I climbed the stairs to bed. I immediately sank into sleep, waking just once. Everyone on earth had died. No. Just my father.

The next morning was bright. Foreign sun shocked my eyes. I called Wendy to tell her. I found my notebook at the bottom of my duffel bag and went to Dad's room. I sketched his coat. Then I did it again. Again. The bend of the long collar and shaft of the arm held a little of the curve of his body. What was the coat doing? It was pulling to earth. I didn't need to do any more than that—just show the tension of gravity against the cloth's faint memory of my father. Just that. Again.

Every day I expected university officials to show up and kick me out but they didn't. I drove my father's Buick to the market. I drank coffee. I bought bread and olive oil, sometimes a piece of salmon. Wendy came over and I baked a big slab of fish in my father's ancient oven and made us a feast. She told me a little about each of her children.

The next day I took out my father's huge wheeled suitcase, filled it with my clothes, the quilt, and my notebooks, boxed my mother's china with the wavy green edge, took the fireplace tools in case I ever had a fireplace, and drove my father's Buick back to Santa Barbara.

About a year after that, An wrote to say he wanted to visit with his wife and baby. I said, "Of course." I cooked for a week. I sent for delicacies. I asked local people if I could borrow the works of An's that they'd bought from him and I set up a little gallery in the deli. The plates were on stands, the vases lined up on a shelf I'd cleared of liqueurs.

Ling wanted a tour of the apartment. She wore patent leather shoes and a stylish linen suit. She worked in textile design for a large fabric house in Hong Kong. She had full, curved lips, a clear brow, and a slight Mandarin and French accent, finishing words with a pleasant drop of her voice.

She saw my drawings in the bedroom. "I like the cup series," she said.

The cups were done as my father drank coffee with me in the kitchen after he'd dismissed the housekeeper.

Ling turned to the wall by the window. "The people in chairs are complex. Not quite finished. The one of the lady is maybe the best."

An came to the doorway with the baby, who had fuzzy hair standing straight up. For no reason, the baby laughed. An looked on and smiled at his wife and me.

"Ah," she said. "These are the ones to save." Ten attempts at my father's coat. "These show compassion," she said.

Sentimental, I thought, but didn't say. Lately I'd been waiting a little in conversations before cutting people off. Ling was just being nice to her husband's friend, but that counted. "You're bringing your own kindness to the picture," I said as I looked at my work. I'd almost forgotten that in the background I'd included faint suggestions of my father's bureau, the window he'd stared at, the cypress—an entire room. These presences created tension with the dominating coat.

Not listening, Ling kept looking at the sketches. "There's a fight going on. I can't explain. I'd like to take some of these back with me. I have friends at home in Hong Kong. They should see these."

They should? The sun dazzled the metal rim of my desk lamp. Joyous, southern sun. In my confusion, I blurted, "I've finally learned that drawing is just graphite on paper."

She smiled. "OK then." A pause.

An, my friend, holding his baby, studied the last drawing in the row. "Tender graphite," he said.

LISTEN

arta Holmen's sister Iggy was coming for a visit. Marta washed the kitchen and bath towels in case one of them was stale or dusty, cleaned up stacks of work files on the dining room table, and bought a new lamp from Dorman's for the guest bedroom. She bought a drawing from a local deli/gallery and had it framed. Marta hadn't seen her sister in seven years. Iggy, a certified, well-tested genius, was hard to reach or predict. Maybe you said the wrong thing; you'd never know. Iggy would frown and leave the room. Marta was now thirty-four, an attorney who could guide her clients through an intricate divorce. Her sister brought her back to being a kid caught up short and tongue-tied.

Marta brought her guitar out of her bedroom and propped it in the corner of the kitchen so Iggy would notice it. See she was learning something new.

It was a Saturday in June, unusually hot. Marta sat on her front step in baggy shorts. She generally liked living alone with only the occasional grad student from UC or a touring musician to share her pillow. This Saturday before Iggy's visit, the house felt too clean, empty. Almost soul-less. She looked through her three Monterey pines to downtown Santa Barbara. She could just see the historic courthouse, a few streets. No songbirds. Sometimes this silence gathered in the late afternoon, and Marta wondered if it was because owls came out to hunt. Did they eat songbirds? Divorce lawyers?

She drank two tablespoons of lemon juice over ice with no sugar, Iggy's sour creation of many years ago. Marta was restless—fearful? *Afraid of the past*, she thought, clear as day. Not her style. The low sun spread a sheen over the town, picking out a few windows as distant mirrors.

Every life had hidden nodes of anguish and her own set of difficulties—a strange sister, a blind father, the dishonest man who read to him, a mother towering with bitterness—were different only in the details. Those details—like wispy ghosts—had begun to braid her thoughts.

She'd considered writing down a few of the incidents. In her job, she was good at gently squeezing out the anguish of divided families, setting their pain aside, and writing down precise descriptions of assets and terms of agreement. It was gratifying to help people organize their chaos. What is; what is not. What will be; what will not be.

The bulk of the sun hid behind the low trunk of the farthest pine. There was an eerie, forgetful gap in her past that she felt as a kind of longing. Or maybe she'd just missed her sister all these years. She *had* missed her. The childish ache of trying to talk to her sister came back. She went inside, sat at the desk in her bedroom. There was a pen in her hand. How did that happen?

BEFORE MARTA TURNED ELEVEN, her mother Ella, who

thought it was a form of respect to apply her acid humor to children as well as adults, said with a little laugh, "Ah, a tween. Such an ugly word." She ran a palm up over stray hairs at her temple. "May as well say 'over the hill.'"

"Guess there's no hope for you," Marta said to her sister.

Iggy looked up from her book, waited five beats, then said, "Touché," the delay making it seem like the start of something, not the end. Marta didn't know what to say.

She and her sister had three hours before the afternoon's reading session. They were required to spend a half hour listening to Franklin, a former graduate student, read to their father. Thursdays were late so that Franklin had time to get through the traffic after teaching his class *Beyond Assimilation* at UW.

Marta raced out the door. A breeze from Canada had brought heavy clouds that were a tight lid over the Seattle sky. She shivered but didn't want to go back for a jacket. She planned to go downtown and steal something. What? She wasn't sure. Tomorrow, she would get presents and maple bars from the shop near her mother's dental office. She didn't crave anything. Her thoughts careened. It had to be big. A diamond from Nordstrom's. She could slip it off the counter when the clerk wasn't looking. Or a ruby. Which was more important—a ruby or a diamond? She didn't know why or ask why. Iggy was the original thinker, according to their father, not Marta, the one who examined other people's ideas.

She was past the neighbor's big fir tree when Franklin's Subaru showed up. He parked at the curb in front of the fire hydrant, as he did every dawn and afternoon. Franklin, the reader, the man whose deep, unwavering voice saved her father from giving up after his accident, the man her mother called "the *lifeline* of the family," without any sharpness. He was tall and wore a thick peacoat. He didn't see Marta. Franklin. A heaviness came over her.

The bus arrived, its brakes wheezing, and Marta swung in. She used her mother's pass even though her own school card would have worked just as well. She liked taking things from her mother's purse, then slipping them back in. As the trees sped by, she thought of Franklin's hand on the small of her back, and a sense of being crowded came over her. Why were all these people riding the bus in the middle of the day, talking, laughing...breathing. She put her backpack on the empty seat beside her. Generally, she didn't think of Franklin outside the reading room. The well-kept, big-leafed trees near the zoo were perfect, like cartoon trees, but even they looked crowded, uncomfortable.

The new Nordstrom had wide, clean escalators and shiny floors. The old one had smelled comfortingly of shoe polish and the wintry-ness of wet wool, even on a sunny day. One carousel held fake silver and diamond earrings. Three teenagers were picking up the jewels on their cardboard backings and holding them up to their ears. The clerk glanced up from a customer and smiled at the girls, practically telling them to steal something. Why didn't the clerk call security? Because there was nothing valuable here. A sense of "who cares?" came over Marta, which she hated. It was a mood that came more and more often, telling her she was getting older. She was sliding into the land of who cares. Who cares if you steal glass? Adulthood loomed—her life going from diamonds to glass. Her heart started to pound. She thought of her mother, fourteen years younger than her father, sighing in front of the bathroom mirror before heading to the office. Her mother would reach back to hook the gold chain necklace looped through her wedding ring. She'd absently rub lotion on her clean hands. Who cares if your mother hates fixing teeth all day? Who cares if your mother pictured a completely different life, playing mahjong in the afternoon, her famous husband on her arm at night, the two of them dancing at faculty parties? Marta felt dizzy. The store elevator creaked upward behind her.

The sickness would pass if that stupid clerk would quit smiling.

Marta tried to stand tall, to think of air between the segments of her spinal cord, like Iggy told her to do. Into her mind came a picture of their father slouching in his soft leather chair, becoming one with the chair while Franklin read to him. Franklin again. The pink carpet in the store made the air pink, unbreathable. Her father was a sociologist. Each year since the bike accident that blinded him, he'd shrunk, his old sweaters folding around him. Every year, citations to his work dropped, requests to be on panels slowed to a trickle.

Entropy man, Marta thought and anger rose, somebody's anger. A mist of anger that cleared her mind a little. The clerk turned and fiddled with things in a drawer. Franklin once read twenty pages of a monograph on entropy before Dr. D. waved his hand impatiently. "Enough. Move on. Move on."

Marta walked up to the clerk, who turned finally. The clerk was too old for the purple lipstick that matched her nails. Marta said calmly, "That redhead has two pairs of earrings in her purse."

IGGY WAS READING, SITTING cross-legged on her bed, which was at right angles to Marta's bed. "Wha's up?" Iggy said, her way of being funny though she didn't look happy.

Bright spots made her cheeks feverish. She turned a page with a shaking hand. Iggy had passing nerves that no one understood.

Marta said, "I went to Nordstrom's to steal something."

Iggy looked up. Even her eyebrows and lashes were blond, making her dark eyes seem to flash under the mildest circumstances. "To see if you could?" A spark of interest, rare these days.

"Something like that."

Iggy shrugged. Had she been crying? Since skipping fourth and fifth grade, Iggy had been preoccupied. Their mother said the bullying would stop as soon as the kids got used to her. Iggy said, "They have people in plain-clothes that look like anyone."

"I know." Marta didn't know. The clerk knew. The whole world knew. "*You've* never stolen anything."

"Haven't I?" Iggy went back to her book. End of subject. No one would ever know what was bothering her.

At sixteen—in three years—Agnes Ignacia (Iggy) Holmen would graduate from the Seattle Academy for Gifted Youth and, as the sisters' mother said, bolt to the other side of the world. Iggy's final escape. She got the Academy counselor to arrange an individual study abroad program in Sweden, learned to speak Swedish fluently by watching her host family's subtitled American TV programs, talked her way into a mechanical engineering program at the tuition-free University of Stockholm, then worked on improving safety on oil rigs in the North Sea.

Some of the experts their mother had consulted when Iggy was young said that she was on a spectrum. One explained that extreme intelligence and being at the edge of the bell-shaped curve were often indistinguishable.

Marta thought of her sister as a moth in an overturned glass bell—like an empty cake cover—flying here and there, full of moth plans, almost oblivious to anyone looking in. Sometimes Marta tapped on the glass just to see if Iggy would look up.

She didn't.

Marta climbed out the small window by the extra bookcase, bracing herself in the niche between the two gables away from the wind, her place. The cherry tree rose two stories to the gutters. Mount Rainier was hidden behind pillars of iron clouds toward the southwest. Minutes passed. She imagined rolling into a ball and flying off to the mountain that no one could see.

And then it was time for the reading. Marta turned on the steep, uneven shingles to grasp the sash. Where was Iggy? Evaporated. Gone. A genie back in the bottle.

Not in the reading room either. Franklin was at his usual corner in front of the sloping backside of the staircase, marking his place with two long fingers. Marta wasn't afraid of him; she didn't know why, but as she nodded to him, there was something, a solidifying in her heart. He wore a plaid shirt, loosened cloth tie. He told Marta once that his wife, Tina, picked out all his ties. Marta knew that Tina existed but it was hard to remember. Tina sometimes got bit parts in the Green Lake Community Theatre. She wore dresses that were too long and liked to quote old movie stars. Marta's mother called her "Madame" behind her back.

In the reading room, Franklin nodded back to Marta. He had a long face, a sharp jaw. The afternoon's stack of magazines and reading materials were in the alcove behind his left shoulder, the C-shaped stand that he used as a mini-desk angled over his lap. His long legs in cheap wool stretched into the little room. Marta went around them and gave her father a kiss. "Where's Iggy?" she asked.

"Basketball." Crevasses edged her father's cheeks and curved past the corners of his mouth. "Extra practice." He smiled in her direction. "So you're the entire daughter contingent today." His smile weakened. For years, he'd commanded his daughters to listen to Franklin read *The Times*, the *Proceedings of the American Academy of Arts and Sciences*, the newly discovered letters of Abigail Adams. He said it was good for them to hear the world's business in intelligent form. Even if they didn't understand it completely, they would absorb good analysis and eloquence. It filled Marta with other people's words, a grab bag of opinions that made her unsure of what she thought about anything. Except she knew that her father was lonely. Without an order, his daughters would leave him high and dry, and he'd be alone with hardly any friends and a disappointed wife who was halfway out the door. This was his fear. Marta was the only one who could see it.

Franklin patted the place beside him for her on the bench. Even before she sat down, he picked up reading where he'd left off. His deep, heavy voice brought a steady cadence to the 1997 report from Harvard's Special Y2K Committee.

Marta sat on the bench. The pink air from Nordstrom was in her lungs. She had to breathe shallowly to stay alive. Outside of the reading room, Franklin barely existed. The man with the old leather briefcase rushing up the front stairs twice a day and the Franklin inside the reading room were completely different. As he read, he was an immoveable presence, like a pillar in the center of the room. Marta wasn't sure when he had taken possession of her. Maybe she'd always belonged to him. There had always been his touch in the reading room whenever Iggy had something else to do. Franklin's voice, never stumbling, nothing else happening, only the news of the world, his free hand on the small stand in front of him, expertly turning the pages. His other hand on her jeans thigh gently sliding to her belly. Not a thing happening. His voice continuing, continuing. Marta was a ghost sitting next to Franklin, her father across the room, sunk in his own thoughts, innocent. Marta existed and did not exist. Franklin's voice. His hand. His fingers working the button of her jeans.

Franklin slid his fingers under her panties and gave the slightest sigh, like a pause to emphasize a point. He glanced quickly at Dr. D., whose head was bent, his hooded eyes almost closed. Oh.

Oh. Marta saw the glance as if she had looked down from the low ceiling. There was a girl. A girl still as death. Franklin. Her father listening, not seeing. And then she knew without words, for the first time in her life. Franklin needed her father as much as her father needed him. Franklin, who was now a rising star in the sociology department, the protected protégé of Dr. D., needed Dr. D. in some terrible way that had nothing to do with the department. Everything that happened in the reading room—the awful sense of blooming under Franklin's palm, the dooming charge of her body leaning toward him, hating something, hating, wishing—all that was Franklin's show for Dr. D. A sly, hidden display. Franklin getting away with it. She was beside the point, one of her father's favorite phrases. Beside the point. Without weight. Without mass. No force to hold things together.

Franklin's voice. His hand moving lower. It was the looming Y2K. If you didn't think about it, it didn't, wouldn't be about to happen. Happening. Now, deep inside the world somewhere. Planes would fall out of the sky. No, they wouldn't. That was just in the imagination of people who didn't really know. Who knew?

MARTA, OLDER NOW, STOPPED writing. Her legs brought her to the porch. She slid down to the floorboards, her back against the siding. She'd never forgotten. She had forgotten. She wasn't there. She was.

THE DAY ARRIVED WITH a light breeze and bits of high, white clouds scudding past the sun. Iggy, who had gone through Customs in San Francisco, had insisted on taking a Lyft from the Santa Barbara airport, no reason, vintage Iggy.

She was coming from her home in Tanzania. After her civil service in Sweden, Iggy had wandered the world for six months, then texted Marta that she and a Tanzanian architect were raising funds for a new college. The college, designed by the architect and built with Iggy's crews, trained local men and women to develop roads, sewer systems, and other infrastructure badly needed in poverty-stricken Tanzania. Marta read this online in the literature for Iggy's NGO, called the Tamaini Tent. She'd looked it up since Iggy's texts were rarely personal, mostly pictures of outlandishly colored flowers and screeds about the political situation in the new capital, Dodoma.

Iggy stepped out of the Honda in a blue dress. A dress! She picked up one suitcase that looked new—not her usual shabby, strapped trunk—and walked smiling up the small grassy hill.

"You're tan!" Marta exclaimed. Completely wrong. Instantly, the chattering little sister, but Iggy didn't take advantage. She kept smiling!

"Ya, once the color of a jellyfish, now a tanned jellyfish." She looked at her forearm as she took the last steps to the edge of the porch, then threw both arms around Marta in a tight hug.

Marta squeezed her eyes shut. Ah, Iggy, at last. The one thing Marta had always known was that she was Iggy's sister, crazy Iggy, a North Star shining down on all the trivial mysteries of ordinary people.

Iggy didn't let go. Generally, she would wait through your clasp, then awkwardly pat your back. The relief flooding Marta suddenly turned like a tide that's hit a dike. What was wrong? Was Iggy sick? Oh. The sudden visit.

Marta hung on. She didn't want to know. She did. In their brief phone conversations, she was always the last one to say goodbye. She stood back. "Everything okay?" she asked. The sisters stood looking at each other, suddenly shy.

"Fine. Good. The guy in Customs just wanted to know why I didn't have any more luggage. I guess he didn't have enough to paw through." Iggy glanced out to the pines. "This is beautiful. I should have come sooner."

"The last time we saw each other..." Marta could hardly remember how to bring words out of her mind.

"That awful day."

Their father had died suddenly of pneumonia soon after Marta got into the Santa Barbara law school. A high school friend arranged for one of the rooms at the Burke Museum on campus for the memorial, but it was after the semester and hardly any of his colleagues or former students showed up. The Seattle day was sodden; inside, there was a sound of dripping. Marta and Iggy huddled together in front of intricate paintings on the walls.

Afterward, their mother said she needed a martini. Iggy had a flight the next day to Mombasa.

But here was Iggy, in Santa Barbara, more substantial than ever—taller?

In the entry, Ziggy paused in front of the new drawing. A coffee cup. "Where did that come from?" She frowned. Her concentration, as ever, like a stun gun.

"Someone local."

"That cup goes bottomless where the tea leaves should be."

Marta felt herself shrink. "There's pain." A pause. "I thought you'd like it."

Still musing. "An invitation."

"I wish you liked it."

A long pause. "I love it."

Life returned.

They sat at the kitchen table drinking local beer recommended by Marta's brew snob friends for anyone who loved hoppy beer, which Iggy did. She held out the bottle, read the label, and said it was just spicy enough. Marta's spirits soared. Her sister talked about her apartment in Dar es-Salaam, the art shows and fashion shoots just a few blocks away, gang graffiti in the other direction, Iggy's attempts to collar politicians and get them to support the college, the dancing and singing at the inauguration of a road in a northern province built by one of her crews.

Marta listened with the feeling of watching people and things flying past. Franklin turning a page. No. She'd think about him later. When she and Iggy were young, they never talked about Franklin. It wasn't a decision to talk about him or not—it just didn't happen—but now Marta felt their silence as an astonishing vacuum. Her mother had said once that Franklin gave up teaching. Did he leave for some farm in Finland? Marta got up for another beer, leaned on the sink, her mind racing. Tomorrow would be soon enough to talk—after all this time, she shouldn't spring it on her sister too fast. Iggy was so different! It was wonderful to see her. She looked happy!

Iggy turned in her chair. "Are you listening?" she asked gently.

"Wait. That's my line." So strange to have Iggy in front of her, the past hovering.

The sisters smiled quickly at each other. There was a long pause.

"What's that?" Iggy pointed at the guitar.

"My Fender. They make them for beginners."

"What do you know?"

"That it takes a lifetime."

"No, really."

"Oldies. Taj Mahal. Like that."

Iggy nodded. "Play something."

"Not yet." A pause. "I like having it in the house. Even the case."

Iggy thought about that. "Ya. Potential."

Their quick language with each other. "That one has held onto most of its potential so far."

Iggy laughed, shrugged. "You may be good."

Marta came back to the table with two bottles and popped off the caps. "I was just thinking about the time we took that stuff from Madame."

"And got caught," Iggy said, catching foam with her tongue. "What idiots." She laughed again.

"It was the day after my birthday. You were humoring me. I wanted to commit some kind of crime for some reason, and you said okay."

"I wasn't humoring you!" She touched her face and took a calmer sip from the bottle. "You said we had to take something from Madame. Who else had anything exciting?" Her smile faded with a thought.

"I said that?" Marta felt a near-memory flash by, the flash of a shooting star, then the darkness of wondering if it was real. "Why would I want something from Madame?"

"You said... You wanted to create balance in your life. Some yin for the yang, you said. You know you were a weirder kid than I was." They sat in silence for a minute.

Iggy wore a metal necklace made of hooked rectangles. It shifted on her collarbone as she took a breath. "You broke the window in the laundry room door."

Another flash. "Is that how we got in?" Marta's mind was a vacuum pulling on something.

Iggy rolled her eyes. "Ya. You were possessed."

She was back from whatever had distracted her, happy again to be in Marta's kitchen. Marta pushed open the old casement window a crack for the late-day breeze. Everything else could wait.

They told the story to each other. Creeping through the house looking for something to take. Madame's de-barked cockapoodle leaping up the steps with them. The bedroom with the massive bed and rows of perfectly placed pillows. Then there was Madame's little, blue study at the back—powder blue carpet, blue walls, and a navy blue desk next to her white vanity, the mirror surrounded by a row of lights, a little sink in the corner. A mirrored closet ran along the length of the room. They slid it open and there were Madame's silk tunics, wide pants, and then spangly dresses with a row of spiked heels on the floor. The girls had never seen Tina in the sequined dresses.

Almost a physical hunger came over Marta. She reached for the red one.

"Wait," Iggy said. "Take a picture with your mind so we can put everything back."

"*You* take it. I'm busy." Marta pulled the dress on over her head as the silent dog leaped frantically beside her. Cool cloth encased her and puddled slightly at her feet. She lifted the skirt, lengthened her spine. She looked in the mirror, expecting her little flat face, but there were angles under her cheeks and big eyes. When had that happened? The sparkles of the dress shifted as she turned. She was somebody else, not herself, a red rocket. She could blow something up.

She turned in the other direction. She could tell people what to do. Cut off their heads. Gouge out their eyes. She bent and threw a shoe at the dog, who went clattering down the stairs. The right strap fell off and she pulled it back.

"Wow," Iggy said. "Transformation."

In the kitchen, at that moment of the telling, Marta's mind shot off in another direction. She saw Iggy's pale child's face one evening after Marta had gone ice-skating with a friend. Iggy had been left to do the afternoon reading session by herself. Another time, Marta had a swim meet in Tacoma, and the bus left early on a Thursday. Marta came home to find her sister obsessively stuffing most of her clothes in bags for Goodwill, saying that people in the first world had too many possessions.

Iggy. Of course, Iggy, too. The kitchen in Santa Barbara stood still. There was a far-off tinkling of the neighbor's wind chimes. Iggy first in everything. How could Marta have thought she was the only one? Where had she been? Where had she been?

Slanted afternoon sun barely touched the Formica of the table. It would soon be gone. Iggy went on with the story, caught up in the memory. "My dress was blue. Satin, I think. Probably polyester!" She shook her head with a smile and talked about how they'd gone marauding over Madame's little crystal bottles, vials, and packets on the vanity, doing each other's makeup in ways that they'd read about in old copies of *Elle* and *InStyle* in their mother's waiting room. "The modern woman likes a bold brow," Iggy had said as she dipped a wand into a domed bottle called *Thrive Instant Fix* and turned Marta's face toward hers.

"Then Madame showed up!" Iggy continued, laughing. She told the story well. "'How could you!' Madame said, shouting. 'You little thugs. What have I ever done to you?' and you...cool as a cucumber... You nodded toward her closet and said, '*That* is a crime against humanity!'"

"Franklin's wife," Marta said heavily.

Iggy stopped. She looked at her sister. "Yes."

"We were in Franklin's house."

"What's this?" Iggy's face took on the stiff neutral she did so well.

Marta said, "Franklin."

"I see." Iggy nodded, the neutral deepening. Her eyes left Marta's face. A long moment passed.

With a start, Marta realized how dark her kitchen was. She couldn't think in the bleary room. The house was facing the wrong way. Her mind held a small scream telling her she should have listened to the designer friend who'd thought she should tear out walls, take down the pines. What? She said, "I've been thinking about Franklin."

Promptly and quietly, "I don't want to hear it."

Soon, they would be sitting in the shadow of the pines

and the useless, shabby cedar by the driveway. Why didn't Marta take care of things? She said, "You have to hear it."

"Actually not." Iggy sat up straighter.

"Everyone says you should—"

"—what do they know?"

"How can you be like that! No one's like that!"

"I'm like that."

The scream rose. Marta should have re-roofed, painted, sanded the floors! She got up and said calmly, "I wasn't going to do this on day one. I knew this would happen. What's the matter with me?"

"Yes, what's the matter with you?" Iggy said softly. She didn't move. Maybe she didn't know where to turn any more than Marta did.

Okay. Just breathe. Marta rinsed the bottles. "We should go to bed. We'll try again tomorrow."

"No, we won't."

Marta turned. "I can't stand that."

Iggy shrugged, her lips gray.

"I could talk whether you like it or not. I could just tell you whatever I want."

A softening. "I know that."

"So..."

"So nothing."

"Then tell me why." Silence. More silence. "I don't see why." She was pleading.

Iggy lifted the bag at her feet absently, replaced it on the floor. "Because I win as long as I decide." She looked around the room, unseeing. "And I've decided. I've thought about this. No one else sets the terms. No one. Not somebody with a theory." She touched the necklace. "Not you." A long pause.

Marta felt the pause as a weight pulling her down. She

couldn't look at her sister or out the window. She didn't know where to look. She'd missed a heel mark on the baseboard by the door. She would spend the rest of her life waiting for her sister, caught in the breathless, unbearable waiting of her childhood.

The silence deepened. Marta sat down at the little table again. She knew that the evening was painting the town below the hill in silver. The change in light would go on without her to see it, of course.

Finally, her sister gently patted the table in Marta's direction. "Franklin's voice," Iggy said. "Poof." She flicked her fingers.

Marta looked up.

"He doesn't get a say."

Marta pressed her knuckle across her mouth. She squeezed her eyes shut. Iggy had said his name. There was that. She moved the cocktail napkin from the brewery. Was it enough? Who knew, but here was her sister, older, smelling faintly of lavender, smoother, as if someone had patted her all over with a fine powder.

The evening breeze crept under the sill. Marta had made blueberry sweet bread for breakfast, her sister's favorite. She thought of the slight waft of pleasure she'd feel as she unwrapped it. Her mind slowed.

She pictured the bread sitting behind the milk in the refrigerator, a tiny, hidden gift. She lost track of the long, long pause.

Finally, Iggy said, "Can I tell you something?"

"Is that fair?" Marta smiled.

"No." She placed one long hand over her other one on the table. "I'm in love."

"Just like that!"

"I know." Iggy lifted a brow. "I don't seem like the kind."

"I mean..."

"I'd told myself I wasn't going to spring it on you the first day. Like..."

"Who is it?"

"He's here."

"Here?"

"He flew in with me. He's staying downtown tonight. I told him I wanted you to myself for a while."

"He's... Who?" Was this supposed to happen?

"Belgian." Iggy rubbed one hand over the other. "But we forgive him that."

Marta was speechless. Iggy had crossed the desert before her.

In the silence, Iggy said, "He teaches math. He's impossible. Like me."

"An impossible Belgian." Her sister was not alone. She was a new element on the earth.

"He's coming tomorrow. At two." A little smile. "I was going to tell you at breakfast."

"Here?" She couldn't quite awaken.

Iggy nodded. "To meet you." She pulled her phone out of her bag. She had his picture on the first page. There was a man in a T-shirt and rumpled shorts looking straight at the camera with a little smile. A sense of possibility ran through Marta. He would be in her kitchen. This impossible man.

Iggy also looked at the picture. She said, "You won't like him."

"Who's to say?"

Iggy went on. "But you'll love him." She absently folded the little napkin. "Because you love me."

"I do love you."

Gently, "Isn't that what I just said?"

HAWK WIND

enise was high in the bleachers, away from other parents, coaches. At the sidelines, her son Stephen kept his head down. Yelled at or praised, he was stoic. It broke her heart.

October on a metal bench, a chill wind stirring leaves behind the crowd. She wrapped the Roosevelt High blanket around her, wished she'd brought a cushion. A coach should pass out tailbone pads for football moms.

Stephen limped off the field. She'd missed it! She got up. Sat. Stephen would be mortified if he caught her coming to the sideline. He kept his helmet on. No trainer. He must be OK. Her heart slowed. On third down, they sent him back in.

Since her husband Tom died, her soul left, came back, left again.

In the last minute of the quarter, Stephen misread an option, his man side-stepped, turned to the open field, and Stephen spiked him from behind. The boy flew through the air and hit the frozen ground with a crunch. The crowd gasped.

Everything stopped. The boy didn't move. All eyes on his hands, on the one foot showing past the kneeling trainer and bunches of players. Did any part move? *Please move.* Stephen? There. Standing beside the end of the bench. Arms folded. Head down. Rocking a little from side to side.

Denise pushed past a huge man and tore down the aisle. A roar went up from the crowd. Relieved clapping. She caught up to Stephen and the assistant coach escorting him off the field. "Pack. We're going to the lake."

Stephen towered over her. A boy in a monster suit. "Can't we talk later?" His voice broke with shame, or something else.

She took his arm, knowing that embarrassed him. She had to pierce his world. "You need to think."

He shook his head, but clutched her arm against his side.

THE LAKE WAS AS big and risky as she remembered. Dug out by a retreating glacier, it covered twelve square miles just south of the Canadian border. On a hot day, the top layer of bath water covered tiers of icy depths. One splash and a swimmer was buffeted by fire and ice. The weeds at the shore gave way to stranded boulders and huge, strangely anti-aquatic pines. Tom wanted to make love outdoors on warmed grass. And she might have, too, if there were linens.

Denise and Stephen arrived after dark from their house in Orchard Park and carried their bags up the small hill to the last cabin in the row. The Northern Lights Lodge stayed open in the fall for quail and pheasant hunters.

She'd gotten the last available cabin. She turned on the thermostat and there was a lot of clanking, a little heat. The firewood basket was empty. "I'll call the front desk in the morning," she said.

Stephen nodded, threw his bag in the bedroom. Without unpacking, he brought out to the pier three deck chairs and the portable TV that Denise's husband Tom had bought years ago. The wind came from the north, but Stephen preferred to be outside. He propped the TV on the third chair and he and Denise idly watched a Thursday night football game by starlight, a football cradled on Stephen's forearm. Denise could almost feel Tom's presence, his hand on her back. She fought off the ache of his death. The water below, black in the night, lapped at the pier's hunkered pilings.

TOM HAD LOVED THE shifting unknowns of the lake, the breeze that blew in force from one direction, then the next, and that seemed to Denise to gather smells of roots and algae, animal scat and strange berries from deep in the pine forest. She shivered. Tom would have put his jacket around her shoulders. The moon rippled toward her across the lake, *Tom's lake*. When she swam in it, silky bodies touched her legs. Fish or weeds or goats, she would never know.

The little TV. She didn't even know which teams were playing. Bears vs. Colts, 7 to 7. Had all the moons aligned so extremely that both Chicago and Indianapolis had good teams?

"You cold?" she asked Stephen. The lonely smell of pine pierced her.

His "no" was an almost imperceptible shift of his big shoulders. When Tom died, Stephen quit talking and started growing. In the half year since Tom's death, Stephen had grown five inches and he was now over six feet tall and almost 200 pounds. Sixteen years old. The bones of his face had lengthened and hardened into his father's features. Denise was reminded of continental drift. Stephen was a new, startling world taking shape in the slow undercurrent of ordinary days. *Ordinary* days. So hard to achieve in the crush of living.

Stephen had started lifting weights after the funeral, and this August easily won the starting position as middle linebacker. When not in a game, he kept his gentle ways, his half-smile, his habit of pulling in his head as if pulling back from his surroundings, reserving judgment. That is, he was careful with his strength until recently, when he'd been benched for too many penalties, not just holding or even clipping, but vicious, deliberate face mask penalties.

The announcer said that if the Bears line couldn't hold any better than that, this was going to turn into a blowout.

"The Colts guy is getting through every time," she said. "Number 51."

"I see that, Mom," he said with a roll of the eyes, but she could see he was pleased. His position. He tossed the ball from one hand to the other.

His coach Arne left her a message one afternoon saying that Stephen had yanked a board out of a picnic table in the park near the practice field. When Arne asked why, Stephen said he just wanted to see if he could do it. Arne wanted her to know. There would be a bill for the table.

Stephen came home very late that afternoon to the shingled house on Delano Avenue that Tom had loved. Denise could have moved to someplace with a study and a real dining room, but she needed to hold onto the backyard elms lining the cinder alleyway, the smell of rusty nails and old wool in the attic, her pattern of moving between kitchen cupboards, the sink, the oven as she cooked dinner. Stephen put the keys to his old Camaro on the TV. He was exhausted from his workout, his dark hair damp and flattened. He drank the last of the milk from the half-gallon carton, stood at the kitchen island, hesitant.

She told him about the call. "You want to tell me about it?"

"No." He crushed the empty carton in his hands, flipped it into the recycling.

She considered rinsing it. Didn't.

Finally, he looked at her. He had a straight nose, heavy brows. He'd become handsome; had she known that? He said, "You just shouldn't let people take advantage of you, that's all." Then he turned and went upstairs.

Who? Who would take advantage?

Lights blinked out on the main lodge down along the shore. During a beer commercial, Stephen said mildly, "I thought you hated the lake."

She'd brought him here because it was the last place where he'd been carefree. She was not an outdoor person. Already she longed for pavement, the faintly oily smell of the elevator she took to her job as a chief paralegal in the Sears Tower. She liked her gray cubicle on the twelfth floor, and even in the depths of mourning, got a few moments of satisfaction from how quickly she could stitch together new language with the standard contract elements for her group of partners. She understood contracts, the balancing of interests. A few of the younger lawyers sometimes asked for her advice.

She'd hoped Stephen would talk to her here.

"Not hated," she said, "challenged by."

He gave a snort.

21-7 and only halfway through the second quarter. "Gotta get the ground game going," the announcer said. Jay Cutler tried a keeper, got pushed back eight yards.

Steven looked over, mimicked the announcer's bass. "That line better start holding." He bent a spun the ball on its axis on the wood planks.

She laughed. On summer vacations when Stephen was young, she'd dared herself to appreciate the wonders of the place, like the woodpecker just now hammering bark with alarmingly fast thunks. Shouldn't the bird be asleep? Did he mistake the moon for the sun? Why didn't his head explode?

She turned to her son and said, "Let's go swimming." She could almost make out the black hills across the lake.

"Mom," he said with mock disgust, "I know you're brave." He took a pebble from the pouch of the sweatshirt and tossed it into the lake. The smell of cold water intensified.

Worrying about him was the counter-balance to Denise's grief, she knew. She would have gone mad the last few months if she hadn't needed to be steady for him.

A few days after the funeral, she'd discovered him sobbing in the back yard and had sat on the bench under the elms with him and held him in her arms. In private, she'd howled and spent days staring at Tom's shirts lined up in the closet. Outside, the city buses released their air brakes as if sighing. Neither she nor Stephen cut short their grief, but gradually they stopped referring to Tom in their few talks. Now, when he was mentioned, they both gave a little start. Stephen had been unbearably sad but somehow more all right in the early days. The last few weeks brought a second wave of mourning, a quiet, complicated rage.

28-7. The fake turf at Lucas Field glittered under the

lights. Cutler frowned so hard he seemed cut between the eyes.

They had first come to the lake the summer that Stephen was ten. He was skinny, often running up from the water, shivering, begging Tom to take him out in one of the green canoes lined up outside the dining room of the main lodge. Tom was tall and hefty. They didn't know then that he was the image of what his son would be. Tom would smile, kiss Denise, and pick up the life jackets drying on the cabin's porch rail. This evening when she'd unpacked the car, Denise had seen the canoes on the grass, their paint chipped, a pile of worn paddles nearby.

She hadn't told Stephen about the suicide note, if that's what it was. "Denise, my love, forgive me." No signature. *He must have been planning to say more,* she almost shouted across the lake. *He must have!* How could he leave her with only a careless half-message that she'd crumpled in her hand the moment she found it? It had been in his suitcase.

Late one night last February, Tom, took a train back from Milwaukee after visiting a potential client. He spent much of his time wooing tightly-spun entrepreneurs into deals. Making a match with sometimes Luddite investors on the other side. Tom often said he was built to be a go-between, an explainer, someone who never quit. He would circle and circle and circle until he'd assembled a hole in the clouds, then dive through and land the bird, as he called it, pulling Denise close with a grin.

According to witnesses, a ferocious gust of wind swept through the station at Canal and Madison. Leaning into the wind, Tom lost his balance and fell on a nearby track just as a double engine pulled in. Or else he deliberately walked onto the track. The witnesses weren't sure.

Denise told the coroner, *no autopsy*. This was before the

police released the luggage and she found the note in a zippered side pocket. The coroner said he had no choice, railroad policy. Now Denise was glad for the inquest. The ruling was that the death was an accident. It was official. She would never need to reveal the note to anyone. Her lifelong task, she thought, would be to forget it. And to forgive herself for being oblivious to his turmoil, whatever it was. If only she'd paid attention. Unlike her, Tom was impulsive. She didn't take seriously the moods he slipped in and out of so easily. A familiar mass like a painful dream rose through Denise's heart. There were wisps in the dream, the slightest tense, metallic layer in the clean smell of Tom's sweat months before he died, the way he began to say "OK" a little too fast in their conversations. He reached for her one night and stroked her thigh, his fingers probing before she was ready. Then suddenly he withdrew, gently turned her around and spooned, his hug tight, his breath fast, then catching. "What?" she asked. Nothing, his catching breath against her back. Then, "I just want to hold onto you."

A bootleg. 51—the middle linebacker—read it and felled Cutler with a nice, low tackle. Cutler got up slowly. Denise said, "It must be hard for his mother to watch him get hurt." Dew seemed to be rising from the lake, a layer of chill lifting through the floorboards of the pier. Soon, she and Stephen would go in.

He stretched his feet to the edge of the planks. He smiled, "Very subtle, Mom."

His biggest fear these days seemed to be that she would somehow interfere with his affairs, whatever they were. He gave her only glimpses of his thinking, hints. But he looked so relaxed in his big sweatshirt, his hands stretched out on the metal chair arms, that she said, "You don't bring Julie around anymore." Stephen's girlfriend, a lanky, good natured girl who swam the back stroke for the school's swim team. Her brown hair, often damp from her latest workout, had a slightly greenish tint, a lovely mermaid. Denise liked having another female in the house.

Even when Tom was alive, she'd occasionally longed to have someone in the kitchen who knew the mysteries of the flesh the way she did, the need she thought of as a female longing to stay physically safe, to protect the species. She and Tom had always meant to have another child. Maybe they would have had a daughter.

Stephen smoothed his hands down the long thighs of his sweats. In a low voice, he said, "I found out she's a slut."

Denise held onto her shock, both that he would think that, and that he would say it to her. "Something happened?" She spoke as lightly as she could. If she wasn't careful, he would snap shut.

"She says, nothing." He shook his head with disgust.

"You heard something?"

He turned to her, white spots blanching his cheeks. Denise wasn't accustomed to having a son with such a large face, the heavy bones of his jaw and broad forehead making him somehow unavoidable. The same white sheen appeared when he lifted very heavy weights, lying on his back on the carpet of the bedroom hallway, his brows tight with determination.

He said, "She was seen with somebody." He wiped his hand across his mouth. "Several times." His eyes darkened. "I didn't want to be like you."

Cutler rolled out as if going on a stroll and threw 60 yards for a touchdown! Huge bodies sprawled back at the line of scrimmage.

Denise asked, "Me?" This vacation was for him—why was he attacking her?

He looked away. That damned lapping was incessant. The woodpecker wouldn't let up.

Stephen said, "You know Dad had a girlfriend."

The painful dream came back. Tom had cried. Oh.

She spoke evenly to her son, "What a strange thing to say." Rage beat against her habit of protecting him. Her pulse was a thud in her chest. She'd been so careful not to interfere with *him*.

He got up, bent, and snapped off the TV. Suddenly she was aware of crickets. "Don't act surprised," he said. "You *knew*. You treat me like a little kid."

Did she know? Tom was dead. They had loved each other.

Stephen stood up, his lightweight chair rocking back, knocking the football. He loomed over the end of the pier. He turned and viciously whipped a pebble into the lake. It soared so far that Denise wasn't sure she heard the splash down. Without looking at her, Stephen rid the earth of another pebble, pivoting on his foot. When had he picked up the rocks? For a moment, Denise felt as if he was as strange to her as the lake.

The crickets roared. Denise was freezing. She said to her son, "You're mad because your father left you so suddenly." That had to be it. "You want to find a reason for being mad. That's not surprising. You want to make your father wrong." Keep calm. Let him speak, get this off his chest. *This fantasy.*

"He *was* wrong!" he shouted. "I met her. More than once. Friday afternoons when you were at work." He lifted his chair with one hand and for a moment, Denise thought he was going to toss it into the lake. Instead, he slammed up

one arm and the chair collapsed. He scooped up the football and tucked it under his arm.

"Don't shout," she said. "The water carries." Don't talk.
Don't say it. Please.

She rose and with trembling hands, pushed at her chair
until it gave, then carried it down the pier away from her
son.

He followed, hissing, "The first time I was upstairs
on the computer. It was before Christmas break. I came
down. Dad got stiff and weird. Something was up. I didn't
get it at first. Her name was Elizabeth something. He said
he thought I was at weight training. He didn't even know
we didn't have weight training on Fridays. He kept pulling
up the back of his collar. Stupid, like his shirt didn't fit. I
didn't understand his nervousness. Now I figured it out."

She stepped off the pier to the muddy grass. He took
her arm. "So don't treat me like an idiot."

No. She shook him off and climbed the hill. She crossed
the small porch and swung open the door to the cabin. She
propped the chair against the sofa. Careful. She flicked on
the lamp with seashells glued to its base. Seashells?

Stephen came in behind her, dropped his chair with a
clatter, and sat heavily on the plaid couch, one foot on the
heavily lacquered coffee table. He glared at her.

Denise felt crammed into the kitchen area with its
warped linoleum counter and tiny gas cook top. He took
up so much space! She didn't want to sit down. Her reflec-
tion in the window. Her hair was wild against her neck.
The cabin was made of real logs and puffs of dew-scented
air came through the chinks. A large animal was breathing damply on the little house. She yanked off the top of
a chipped enameled teapot. The top flipped out of her
hands and spun on the counter with a clatter, and she

trapped it under her hand. She couldn't make anything work! *Elizabeth. Elizabeth? Tall?* She came to the funeral at the massive Presbyterian Church in Evanston where Tom's mother lived. Denise splashed water into the pot. She dimly remembered a blue dress, narrow face, shiny, straight dark hair. There was a warm handshake with two hands on hers, a tiny note to herself that this woman with the thin cheeks had come alone. Had her mind's camera recorded the image, stored it? In confusion, she viciously opened the under-counter refrigerator, glimpsed the orange juice, milk, and cheese she'd bought for Stephen, and slammed the door shut with a hard thud of the old insulation around the jamb.

She said, "We forgot the TV."

"The TV? That's your answer?" He winced, shook his head. "Dad conned you, and you just let him. Even now you're letting him! I just want the truth."

She spoke above her smoldering heart, "She must have been a client." She must have been! "The truth is that Dad brought a lot of clients to the house, made them a drink, tried to get to know them outside of business so the business would go more smoothly." A ringing numbness blocked her ears. *Truth?* Denise felt herself peering at the past, all the pieces that could be true. She remembered Tom's strong back, no shirt under the vest, as he paddled the canoe toward the far shore. Young Stephen was sprawled over the bow, his hand trailing in the glassy water. She stood on the dock, her bare feet alive to the smoothness of well-worn, dry boards. Her men before her, she felt a gathering happiness, even as the lake seemed to boil about twenty feet out, as if a monster in the deep was turning over.

"He had clients!" Stephen brayed back. He lifted a stack

of magazines from the table and slammed it back down. "That's all you have to say? He took me to lunch with her at The Arno. He put his hand on her back. Low. He thought I didn't see. Later, I told you Dad took a lady to lunch, but you weren't listening."

Low? Their way? Stephen was mistaken about that. Elizabeth had to be just a client, like all the clients who came to Tom's funeral. They told affectionate stories of Tom's penchant for walking, often tramping miles to visit them across town; of the giant strawberry daiquiris he made; of his trick golf shots, his ability to hit a drive with a putter. Their testimonies had seemed to Denise as if they were in a language she didn't quite know. Stephen sat beside her in the pew. He was fifteen. His eyes were so wide they must have hurt. He'd combed his hair straight back so he looked like someone else's child. He let Denise take his hand. He was under water, the shiny black beacons of his eyes watching her and the others swim past. Had he noticed Elizabeth in the blue dress, standing quietly back by the church door that led downstairs to bible study classrooms?

Denise put a hand to her throat. She was astonished that her mind had quietly tracked the woman.

"We're both tired," she said. "Things look different when you're tired. When you wake up tomorrow, you'll realize you're confused."

He sneered, "You're the one who needs to wake up, Mom." He grasped the pole of the nearby floor lamp and gave it a little shake.

Such meanness. She turned and shouted, "Why are you doing this to me? Why now? If you think I was hurt, why hurt me again?"

"Because you do this dumb act for me, and I don't need it anymore."

"Dumb act?" The tea whistled like a siren. She pulled it off the burner.

"You know, love of the century, you and Dad."

Anger struck hard, a pain in the chest.

He said, "I have a right to know. I am a man."

"Well," she said evenly, "I have a right not to know."

"See. See! You think so, too."

"What about respect for the dead?" He'd reduced her to whining. "Dead" hung in the air. She found a small box of teabags in the cupboard and jammed one into a mug.

Stephen picked up a magazine from the floor. "I lost respect for him when I figured him out."

"Don't say that! He's your father."

He rolled the magazine as if looking for something to hit. "When we get back, I'm going to find Elizabeth. I know she's from Milwaukee."

From Milwaukee. Oh God. "I forbid you," Denise said quietly.

He looked at her across the little dark room. "Mom, I'm sixteen."

She grasped the mug. The rage subsided a little. He sounded so young. The numbness seemed to have spread to her arms, hands. She could hardly feel the heat of the cup as she filled it.

"I have to," he said softly.

"I know," she said. Just moments ago, hadn't he been a little boy watching her every move?

He got up and turned to the dark bedroom in the back. As he left, he said quietly, "I just don't understand why you want to live a lie." He shut the door.

Denise's bedroom was at the front of the cabin. She tried to sleep. The firm mattress seemed to resist her, as if she were sleeping on a table. The moon, which had earlier seemed stuffed with meaning, now looked flimsy and thin. It rose high and silvery over the lake. She closed the green curtains that had a pattern of little pheasants. Something barked, not exactly a dog. The nights were always hard. At home, she couldn't decide whether to leave Tom's pillow on the bed or not. It held the smell of his skin, like a fresh leaf. Finally, she put the pillow, unwashed, on the window seat.

Now, with a start, she remembered arguments with Tom as if they were news from afar. She suggested that he take his mother to church instead of going golfing with his buddies and he shouted back that his mother was none of her business. In fact, she envisioned the three of them taking Stephen to brunch after church and eating blueberry blintzes at Solomon's Deli down the street from the science and industry museum, something other families did. Tom was mad one moment, repentant the next. He teased her about her stodginess and she yielded to his weekends of golf, his late nights working, his vacation plans. She sat up.

With sudden certainty, she knew that Elizabeth was CEO of a software company in Milwaukee, one that continuously processed precise measurements for digital microscopes, lasers, and other equipment that finely diced the world beyond the naked eye. What an odd, detailed thing to remember. Tom must have told her that in idle conversation, when he thought she was barely listening. Did he think of touching Elizabeth when he talked about her business? Was he daring Denise to become alert and catch the way he pinched his upper lip just after he said "Elizabeth"?

Denise curled down against the pillows in anguish. Tom had said he had a meeting with the company's lawyers and would stay in Milwaukee overnight. Denise barely listened, he was gone so often. Did he and Elizabeth argue that night? Was that why he returned early, on the last train out of Milwaukee?

Tom prized loyalty. Almost every month, he had lunch with two guys he knew from Cordell Hull Elementary a mile from their house. He had a network of friends who'd referred business to him for a decade. What if, thought Denise, he betrayed me, and then lost Elizabeth? He'd feel foolish, left with nothing. He wouldn't wait for the horrid feeling to pass.

She got up. The moon turned the curtains chartreuse. She was drowning. She knelt to Tom's suitcase on the floor. She'd used his; it was bigger. Almost to her surprise, she found the wrinkled note in the zippered pocket. She didn't remember putting it back. It was on gray hotel stationery. Had she half-expected someone to write on it while she wasn't looking? Yes. Yes! A larger message for her to hold onto. The boxy handwriting of the single sentence seemed to taunt her. *You're getting nothing from me. Nothingness. And in return, you must forgive me or you'll turn bitter, harsh, the way you were with Stephen today.*

The cabin smelled of smoke and Varathane. Denise had to get out. She put on a jacket over her nightgown and quietly opened her bedroom door. By the coffee table, she picked up a sofa pillow that had fallen to the floor. She opened Stephen's door. He was rolled in the cotton bedspread, breathing rhythmically. Just an hour ago, he'd exposed his father and ruined her past. She shut the door.

She let herself out of the cabin. The poisonous note was in her fist. She would not leave it loose in the world. She walked to the lake and stood on the pier by the abandoned TV. She crushed the torn piece of stationery into a spitball and dropped it onto the water. It floated. A breeze she couldn't feel scudded it into open water. There was a disturbance of the surface. A fish? It would be looking up at the ball from its watery world, up at suffocating air. Suddenly the ball was gone, eaten, or just swallowed by darkness. There, done. Her son would never know. Denise was empty. She'd expected relief. Stephen's relentlessness had delivered her to hollowness. She'd never feel anything again. *Damn him.*

She and Stephen spent the morning in silence. Denise watched her hands make coffee. She threw out the cold tea. Inside, the hunters' break-action guns were little pops from across the lake. She had the sense that Stephen was also watching her, though he steadfastly kept his head down as he sprawled on the couch in T-shirt and flannel pajama pants, leafing through the well-worn lodge magazine, *Best Flies of 2002.* The football fidgeted at his side like a baby who might be thirsty.

Silently, she handed him a cup of half-coffee, half-milk, three teaspoons of sugar, his morning drink. "Let's lay this aside," she said quietly.

"I knew you'd say that! I just knew it!" He stood up, stormed outside. She heard the chair with wide arms creak with his weight.

The cabin imprisoned her. Her heart was wood. Mechanically, she dressed in the tiny bathroom, sitting on the furry green toilet seat cover, hanging her nightgown on a glass knob of the vanity, then returning to the bedroom and folding it in the suitcase. She would not unpack; they could leave tonight, maybe get a refund. She put on her old sneakers. Tom had never talked her into hiking boots.

At the front door, she said, "I'm going to breakfast." Stephen's big bare feet were on the rail in the morning chill.

He shrugged, his gaze on the lake. She knew that if he starved until noon, he would be even angrier.

"All right, then." She turned toward the main lodge and headed down the main path, looking back at the turn. Stephen stood at the porch rail and threw a perfect spiral pass, a long, long arc, into the lake. She kept going.

In truth, she realized, she wanted to sit with strangers there and eat a poached egg in peace, shake off the night. Maybe she could find a *Tribune* and mold this day back to ordinariness, the way she re-molded her life after the sad, throaty call from the police sergeant at the Union Station. For months, she woke with a lurch at exactly midnight. Finally she took the bedroom landline off the jack and threw it in the big garbage can in the alley. Its absence seemed to soothe her unconscious and she slept through the night. Until last night.

The lake, stirred by a giant hand, slapped against the pilings of the pier, sloshed against the lilies crowded against the curved shore. The shots came in flurries, then long periods of quiet. Deer gutted where they fell, their smell, a freight train of smell, hitting the trees. Could she smell it? She bit her toast. A log floated out from the thicket of weeping birches at water's edge.

After breakfast, Denise walked back to the cabin and stood before her son on the porch. "You're all I have now," she said.

He looked up. In the night, his face had changed, the full lips had become more defined, his eyelids heavier. Her hold on him had slipped. Anguish sifted into her chest. He said, "I know, Mom."

She turned and walked back on the path to the canvas-covered recreation shack and signed her name for two life vests. Then she came back to the cabin.

He caught sight of her and smiled. Without a word, he disappeared into the cabin, and came out in shorts and his sweatshirt. He met her at the canoes, selected two paddles and put them in the cleanest canoe, then dragged it to the lake. She took off her shoes, rolled up her jeans and got in the front. He waded out a few feet, then climbed in behind her to steer. She put on her vest. He left his below the middle seat. She didn't say anything.

She clung to the curved wood sides of the bow. Stephen's strokes were so strong that she felt like they were lurching over the water. The sun behind towering clouds. Where had the clouds come from? A sudden darkness descended on the lake. Flecks of water hit her face. She was glad for their sting. She turned. "You row like an Indian."

He gave his half-smile. "Not PC, Mom. And it's 'paddle.'"

She breathed. OK. Their line of talk was restored. The canoe seemed balanced over the water like a bike being pedaled. If Stephen stopped paddling, would they sink? Denise had been in a canoe only once before, when Tom insisted. They had crept along the shore at dusk, spotting an elk in a cluster of wild rhododendron. The ungainly body of the animal with its cartoonish, out-sized antlers had seemed somehow miraculous. Denise had carefully crawled across the canoe's middle seat and kissed Tom, the canoe tipping with her movement, his laughter.

Stephen said, "Dad was too coordinated to fall."

She could barely hear him in the rush of breeze and so his meaning seemed easier to manage. She shouted over the wind, "We should leave that to the experts." She'd believed in experts once. Those with superior knowledge who woke up in the morning without a raw feeling in their throats or stray pockets of dread pressing on their hearts.

In silence, Stephen pushed the canoe straight toward the center of the lake. She turned to face him and watch towering clouds bathed in sun bunch behind the western hills. He kneeled in front of his seat to get better leverage, his head high, wind molding his sweatshirt to his chest. The shots from the forest quieted, the midday lull. Her unused paddle leaned against Stephen's calf. The downy hairs of his legs seemed unbearably tender.

He was an expert at canoeing, sure of himself, knowing just how to dip his paddle to get maximum force, keeping her safe. She shouted to him, "It's nice to be out here. I feel freer."

The lake slid under her. Clouds filled with lead moved over their tiny cabin. The smell of the lake seemed to come from greener things, as if seaweed were rising to the surface. Denise's heart rose. She imagined her son encased in his football uniform, his helmet. He'd take his stance, his heart pounding, as he waited for the count, the onslaught. He was drawn to danger.

He turned his head and shouted, "If I find out I was right about Elizabeth, you're going to hate me."

She clutched the seat. "What's the matter with you?" Sun shone eerily on the east side of the lake. "We were having a good time."

He turned. "What's the matter with me? Whatever I say, you still don't answer." He stopped paddling and a stillness caved in on Denise as the canoe slowed. Was it sinking? It was so old. The floorboards were wet. There must be leaks.

He dropped his paddle on top of hers. His lips were chapped, as if he'd bit them in the night. The tops of his cheeks were rimmed with gray. He was as scared as she was. "Answer me," he said.

Not today. Not yet. "There's going to be lightning," she said, "I want to go back."

"All right then," he said quietly.

In an instant, he was standing balanced on his seat with feet apart. He bent one knee, then the other, rocking the boat.

Mesmerized, she watched the muscles bunch in his thighs. He held his arms out, eyes closed. He didn't care what happened next.

"Stop!" she cried, though she knew that was useless. She pushed back to the curved aft and tried to lean out over the lake in counterbalance to his shifts. She was no match.

The canoe seemed to rotate as if on a spit. For a moment, Denise was upside down; the lake was the sky. Then cold water enveloped her. She opened her eyes. Icy green murk. The life jacket popped her to the surface and she took a huge breath. Thunder pounded the water. She'd missed the lightning.

Stephen, who was closer to the overturned canoe, pushed a paddle toward her. She took it and he pulled her to the boat. Its curved hull was hard to hold onto. She spread one hand on the rough paint, the other on the paddle.

Stephen held a thick arm over the bow of the boat. He took huge breaths against the cold.

Gasping, she felt the water rock against the sky. For one instant, the bursts of her heart seemed to merge with the swells of water. Terror soared through her; she remembered the absolute thrill of spinning in space, of not being able to turn back. In a flash, she imagined the split second of Tom's horror. No return. She tasted fish and blooming lake weeds. Her throat and nostrils filled with water that had washed over things bursting to die. She looked at her son. He squinted in grief. He needed to hold onto what he dreaded. She said, "I don't know what I'll hate. I'll have to see."

He put a quick hand to his wet mouth that was as shiny as a baby's. Then he let his hand slide to his chest. "All right," he said. "An answer." Water drops clung to his lashes. He was out of breath. "All right." His hand lay on his heaving chest.

She touched his shoulder. The water was getting warmer. He looked across the dome of the boat, but didn't move away. Thunder tore the sky directly overhead. Again, she hadn't seen the lightning. She said, "Out here, we're sitting ducks."

He closed his eyes, opened them. He said, deadpan, "I should have thought of that."

She shrugged, smiled. What would they do?

Suddenly he turned, and with a great kick, heaved himself up on the hull, grasped the far gunwale, and pulled the boat over. It sat low in the water, but floated upright. With another great heave, he pulled himself in, and then seized the shoulders of her vest and dragged her over the side. They lay gasping against the canoe seats. Huge raindrops, surprisingly warm, fell against their faces. They didn't move.

He turned to her. "Remember the year the electricity went out?" He pushed wet hair off his forehead. "Dad chopped wood for the fireplace."

Did she? Her memories seemed to blow in from a different direction now. "Yes."

He was still breathing hard. "He should have taught me how to use the axe."

"Me, too."

A PLACE FOR FINE HATS

ouglas Enns and I had shared his sunny half of a duplex in San Diego's Old Town for about a year. I loved Douglas's slow way of moving. He ate carefully, as if locating each morsel's vital nourishment. He thought things through and talked in a measured, slightly literal way, like a self-driving car. As my 34th birthday got closer, however, we started arguing over small matters—whose turn it was to feed the yellow tabby, whether to plant a camellia or bougainvillea by the mailbox, why I was never ready to go out when I said I would be. He jangled the cars keys. I swept the kitchen floor in my underwear and Bella Belle sandals, declaring that I was almost dressed.

Early one morning, he backed down the stairs from our sleeping loft and I kissed him, hoping he'd forgotten our argument about the Chancellor's ball. I'd changed my mind and didn't want to go to his department's fundraiser.

He kissed me back and said solemnly, "Keep your promises." He was thin and wore the faded robe I loved—I'd never known a man under forty who wore a robe. I burrowed my hands in its deep pockets. Musing: *Deep pockets, ha. The scientist's grail. Anything for a chunk of change to keep from starving.*

I said, "I don't even know why you sign up for these things." I handed him a cup of coffee, and he took the bread out of the toaster, then laid two even pats of butter between them so the butter would melt enough to be smoothly plastered from corner to corner. Our morning routine. But this day, his hand on the counter as he waited seemed unbearably deliberate. I felt like I was being pulled into his slow-motion dream. There was so much we had never done together. The pocket beach at La Jolla, lunch at La Valencia to pretend we were one of the movie stars in the wall photos. Cool shoes. Cooler hats. The Skifari at the zoo to watch giraffes curl their mile-long tongues around leaves in the treetops.

I had my own lab to get to, a new teaching assistant who needed some clarification on protocols for the fourth generation of the crustaceans we studied. Agitation simmered through me. I grabbed the top piece of toast, spooned on raspberry jam. "I don't want to spend three hours of my life with a bunch of wet physicists." I got our orange juice. "Present company excepted." I nudged his arm. "Can't you forgive me?"

"I don't want trouble." His dark hair fell across his forehead, making him look boyish. I pictured him as an awkward kid, a guy who taught himself to move with dignity after reading several books on the subject.

He would leave it to me to make up my mind. I took a bite. To find my dignified center and do the right thing. Which was to come back from a ten-hour day, get into my understated mauve dress by Theory (a pun to amuse myself), and go to a meet and greet with Two-Buck Chuck and donors who treated scientists like mildly interesting (very mildly) specimens.

"No one even dances!" I thought of my mother in San Francisco dressed in silk for the opera and the after-parties. I hadn't heard from her for several mornings, which was unusual.

"Last year Bernie got $400k just by standing around and talking to a currency speculator about all the advancements in spectrometers he wished he had."

"Fun." I lifted my brow.

He gave a little smile.

"I'd like ... " My phone pinged. A text from my mother: *Need help. Unguent.*

My mother was an enthusiastic, careless texter who tended to live from unguency to unguency. I texted back: *Give me a sec.*

I said to Douglas: "I just want to be home with my favorite ... " Ping. *Catch a plan.*

" ... physicist." *Mom, hire a proofreader.*

Hurt. Sad face. President's Day. Need u 4 sale.

My mother owned a hat shop at Kearny and Vallejo that had survived the ups and downs of the Bay economy, two marriages, periodic fashion pronouncements that accessories were dead, and the embarrassment of hat hair. She could make any holiday an occasion. Her flyer for President's Day featured Lincoln and Mary Todd in top hats. Even during an odd holiday in February, she sold grace, optimism and humor with every hat. But it was a lot of work. She was a lot of work.

Got a thing Fri night.
Sunday??? For bday.
Lincoln or me?

YOU!!! Plus a secret. Then a separate text. *Congratulations.* A shower of confetti.

A faint alarm ran through me. My mother didn't usually persist like that. I set out the granola, two bowls. "My mom needs me."

Douglas looked up. "Really needs you?"

He liked my mother despite her tendency to exaggeration. I shrugged. "Hard to know. I think I should go up there."

"We can put off your birthday."

"Easy for you to say." I handed him the white raisins he preferred. Waited a beat. Then I smiled.

His relief warmed my jangled heart.

I HAD A KEY to my mother's condominium in North Beach on Pacific. I stowed my bag on the red leather couch and went out into the heavy mist. I rarely wore a hat and was bareheaded now. I told myself that with my narrow face, I didn't look good in most hats. My hatless state was one of the unacknowledged frictions between my mother and me.

I headed to my mother's shop. When I was young, I helped her most Saturdays, watched her sell a little touch of beauty in this disjointed, eerie world of atmospheric ozone gone awry, exponential species extinctions, diseases fulminating in the bush. She could take an ordinary customer in baggy pants and retro car coat, place on her head an ultra wide-brimmed Patricia Underwood picture hat in plum-colored pressed wool, slide her hand across the front so the brim skimmed the customer's wary eyes, and voilà, a woman who might, according to my mother, become a spy, find the chalice, or sleep with George Clooney.

But after the exhaustion of grad school and my [tense battle—campaign] for a place in a small lab at the Edwin A. Miller Crustacean Institute in La Jolla, my mother's cheery search for a heightened reality began to irritate me. She seemed willfully irrelevant, frivolous, almost impossible for me. I was a serious person. Yeah, I could dougie, but I also had crustaceans to take apart and reassemble.

I visited when I needed a break from method living. The City was almost deserted of real tourists, just bewildered conventioneers with name tags trying to find a quaint café for a short lunch before returning to lectures on orthodontia or underwriting. It was so good to get out of the unrelenting perfection of San Diego weather and into the fog. I had time for a walk.

When I was young, my mother and I had a cottage in Fremont across the Bay, and she took the early train to work. To me, San Francisco was my mother's exotic city, a place where she managed the weight of her business—worrying about such things as the January drop in walk-in customers and how much inventory to keep in the back room. In the shop, she flirted with men and women alike. She was in her early thirties then, but in her flowing pants and silky tunics, she looked much younger. She understood that she was selling allure, and by the time I was fifteen, I knew that she was alluring. The city held for me the tension of my mother's intricate hopes.

I loved its smell of wet concrete and seaweed as I crossed Columbus, the aged glow of neon signs in the pearly gray air, the faint sense of perpetually falling as I descended Grant through Chinatown. My spirits lifted. *Douglas should be here*, I thought, *ascending, descending. He should see what makes me happy.*

The last couple of days at work had gone well. My new

research assistant suggested a way to streamline our data records to compare my research on a particular decapod crustacean with Baylor's current studies of stomatopods.

Douglas would be into his Sunday routine. He ran a path bowing away from the surf, then bowing towards the harder wet sand after the wave had gone. Maybe some work on the garden. He was right that the begonia fit the space by the mailbox better than a wild-growing bougainvillea. I thought of the way Douglas often lit a single candle when we went to bed and yet took care to blow it out just before we fell asleep. He'd gently take my glasses when my Chris Bohjalian novel dropped onto my chest.

The smell of sweetened meat and long-roasted root vegetables filled the air. A thought rose through the mist of my mind, then sank. I couldn't retrieve it.

This was a city always ready, even on a Sunday morning at 11:00, to spring a surprise on an unsuspecting shellfish boffin.

My mother's shop was at the corner of a nineteenth-century building that miraculously survived the 1906 earthquake and fire. I stood outside the mullioned windows and looked in.

She sat at her black-lacquered desk, her chin resting on her knuckles, her fine profile reflected in one of three mirrors on the back wall that highlighted cloches on short wooden posts. She had recently developed a set to her full mouth and a softness at her neck that showed she was almost mid-fifties. She had pulled her streaked blond hair into a low ponytail. She never wore a hat in the shop, saying that she wanted her customers to have a blank slate to work from. She had high cheekbones and a dusting of freckles in the shadows beneath her eyes. She was not pretty. Her features were too bold, her brow too perfectly curved for anything less than handsomeness.

She tilted her chin just so, as if posing for a camera, as if she were in some kind of reality show that perpetually caught her from an outside angle. She looked like a lightly aged, very clean hippie, a natural beauty who longed for some distant fire circle. Her self-consciousness had an innocence to it.

I hesitated for a moment, gathering myself for the blaze of my mother. She had put track lighting just inside the two banks of windows so from the outside, one peered into a forest of glowing Stetsons, fedoras, Malibus, portrait hats, boaters, homburgs, and gauchos. The light shining on feathers and satin bands made the hats seem almost animated. Near the narrow black door to the stock room was a metal sign engraved with Christian Dior's remark, "Without hats, there would be no civilization."

I pushed open the heavy door that triggered a bell and she looked up, a little startled, her long fingers touching her face. "Oh, Nicole, you're here. I was just adding up the time since you landed, and suddenly you appear!"

She turned my arrival into an act of magic. My heart expanded, but then a slight unease set in. She held an elevated dream of me, and I wasn't sure how to fulfill it. Around my mother, I always felt somehow disappointed with myself. She wanted me to have a wonderful connection, the one thing I couldn't do.

This day, I noticed a slight tension in her brow, a genuine relief, maybe, that she had someone to talk to in the deserted shop.

She gave me a long hug. A loose wisp of her hair touched my cheek. Maybe I was the one who was relieved. She seemed ample, forgiving of my disarray, her slightly thick body so different from the sinewy scientists I worked with. They were for the most part likeable women, but they tended to cut short conversations that strayed, and they gave quick hugs, leaning in only with their bony shoulders.

My mother held me away and studied my face. "So tell me, how are the shrimp?"

"We've got our life expectancy up to 9.3 months, which is great in a tank, and I installed some mirrors so we can watch them do it which, by the way, requires him to go at right angles to her side so he can put it in a little pocket she has there."

"I'm glad I asked." She patted my hand. "I think you're supposed to say 'male' and 'female,' dear, or you get kicked out of science."

I laughed out loud. Our nonsense. My mother was the opposite of my serious lover. "But more importantly, what's the big secret?"

My mother's eyes widened. "I thought you'd never ask! I'm in love! I know you think I always pick the wrong man, but this is the one! We're soul mates. You're going to love him. I didn't want to tell you until I was sure, and now I'm sure, and you're here! This is wonderful."

I realized in that instant why I rarely wore hats. I held out a mean little disappointment in my mother for never producing another father for me.

I smiled. "So you've been holding out on me."

She reached out and rubbed my shoulders in her excitement. "I have!" The tension I'd seen before flitted across her eyes. They were green with gold flecks, and the lids seemed heavy for a moment. My mother was prone to migraines, and I wondered if one was coming on. But then she brightened. "His name's Ellis Fournier and he's practical, like you."

My mother, who liked to present her flighty, sweetened version of life, actually had an efficient side. After all, she made a living selling hats even in this hatless era when most Americans wanted to look careless, as if they'd rolled out of bed and stepped into a wind that made them beautiful. As my mother often said, a hat, on the other hand, is a statement announcing that one wishes to live large, to be a Bogart or a Garbo, a Jackie O or Churchill.

In the last few years I'd been living a little small. My mother stepped away from me, her hands slightly raised, her long shantung vest gleaming. She knew that most hats ended up in the closet, but she said this didn't entirely diminish the power of the hat. Even in a box, it brought a little glow of possibility to the owner's life.

I sat in one of two velvet customers' chairs facing her desk. "How did you meet him?" I said.

"Here, of course. He wanted a fedora for black-tie. He was seeing someone, but we made an instant connection." She sat in her desk chair with the high wood back. "We've been practically inseparable ever since."

I thought I was too old to need a father, but a familiar hope rose. Maybe this was the one. But what did I expect? That he would ask me to play catch on a field in Golden Gate Park? That we would have long father/daughter talks about my studies of a shrimp five centimeters long, *Peneaus totecus* to be exact. But why wouldn't he talk about my career with me? Maybe he'd even have insights into why I'd started talking in measurements, like Douglas. Against my will, I felt my mother's ebullience come over me.

"What does he do?" He was probably a slacker who lived

off self-made women like my mother. What was he doing going to black-tie? Didn't he have some work to attend to?

"Fine woodworking. He's in demand all over the city. He has a crew that builds in bookcases and media centers that hide the TVs and makes chests that look like heirlooms."

"He's a carpenter." Earthy. Hardly my mother's type.

She nodded. "I'm tired of the masters of the universe. He makes beautiful furniture and then comes home and has a beer and he's happy. He's a little shy."

My mother with someone who was shy? "But he goes to fancy parties," I said.

"He gets invited to the charity balls that his customers go to. They all love him. Everyone loves him!"

How could I bring up the pettiness of my slow, inexplicable disenchantment with Douglas? I felt mundane and crabby.

She put her fingertips to her chin, a slightly theatrical gesture of deep thoughtfulness. "Don't you believe in love at first sight?"

"I do, mom. But fifteen times?"

She sagged.

I measured my life in coffee spoons. "I can't wait to meet him!"

She gave a luminous smile. "He's coming for lunch! He'll be here any minute." She

went into the back room and quickly pulled a plastic bag of fresh spinach from the tiny refrigerator under a worn, marble counter. I stood at the door and watched her wash the leaves.

When I was a teenager, she told me about the breakup with my father. She found a single earring in the glove compartment of his Stingray. I wondered how my father and his loan officer did much of anything in the narrow seats of a Stingray, but I kept my practical considerations to myself. I could tell that my mother was devastated not just by being rejected, but by being rejected in such a trite, sordid way.

My father refused to wear anything but a baseball cap with the bill folded in an exaggerated curve. She hated baseball caps, saying, "Why does everyone want to look like a bald, failed athlete?"

I'd seen a photo of my father taken in 1986, when I was two, the year he made a fortune on a device to stamp identification numbers on printed circuit chips, then ran off to Kauai with the willowy banker. She had come to San Francisco on vacation. My mother called her willowy. I'd never seen her.

My father didn't come to the mainland very often, and when he did, he arrived alone, unannounced, showing up at my mother's doorstep with a puka shell necklace or something else bought from the Lihue airport for me. When I was five, my father died of a heart attack while body surfing. When I turned twenty, my mother gave me a small packet of letters he'd sent me. They were only a few sentences each, written in all caps—"Today I saw three clown fish and a barracuda. It ate out of my hand." In the picture he wore shorts, a gray T-shirt, and a Giants cap.

THE PHONE RANG. SHE answered it in front. A few words, a pause as if gathering herself, then she came back to the tiny kitchen area and, without looking at me, said quietly, "He got tied up with clients." She winced. "He can't get away." The edges of her fine lips turned gray. I would never have allowed myself such disappointment.

"All the more for us," I said too quickly. Her plummeting spirits pulled at me. She could pull me under.

She was not going under. She grabbed a bag of wal-
nuts from the little cupboard and her arms lifted with a
big breath. "His business is booming! People want the real
thing, something crafted from the heart! That's what he
gives them." Then from the kitchen that was barely big
enough for one person to turn around, she produced our
lunch—salads with nuts, Gorgonzola, and thin slices of
sweet peaches. She had baguettes with slabs of real butter
and for dessert, she poached skinned apples in her micro-
wave and drizzled chocolate on top. We ate at her desk.

After lunch, she called Ellis back and arranged a birthday dinner for me the next evening. OK, his nonappear-
ance was a small slip in plans. Not a tragedy in the making.

I TOLD DOUGLAS ONE night about my mother's passion
for hats and my refusal to wear one. "I should see a shrink,"
I said. I was on my back. The sloped ceiling of the loft
dropped low to the window by my shoulder. I turned and
kissed his damp neck. "I'm a hat virgin."

"Nikki, shush."

"Sorry. I don't know why I chatter after ... "

He lay back against the pillow and pulled me to him,
his arms under my mounded breasts. He said, "You talk to
make up for what isn't there."

Silence. There was one star. Where were the others?

"Well, you don't talk to make up for what *is* there!" Too
harsh. "There, there. A rose is a rose, like that."

"I'm not looking for words." He bent his head. "Or even
sense."

"I give what I have."

"For me."

There was silence. I tried to think of something sooth-
ing, but my mind roved. I was thrilled at eleven to get the

little cupcakes on my chest that signaled my initiation into some fantastic club. But those cupcakes just kept rising. I lost my center of gravity. I still didn't have it. I found Douglas's hand and kissed it, but he was already asleep. Dreaming of summer camp, I thought, s'mores, a Girl Scout toasting him a perfect marshmallow.

I EXPECTED ELLIS TO be a lanky man much younger than my mother, with big hands and bedroom eyes. I got the hands right. He picked us up in his clean GMC truck, and we three squeezed into the cab, Mother in the middle. I glanced around her to him. He was barrel-chested with a wide face and a fringe of gray hair around his bald spot. He wore a tweed sport coat and a tie with tiny figures that curved over his ample stomach. Propped in the cramped luggage space behind the seat was his Tilson. It had a deep dip in the crown and was a pleasing olive-brown color. Rain sluiced against the windshield. Most of my mother's lovers had been gregarious, take-charge, talkative men. Ellis concentrated on the traffic as if he were making his way through a maze. Lights gleamed against my mother's black-beaded pillbox hat.

Finally, he said, *"Un ange passe."* His pleasantly low voice dropped at the ends of the words, as if he might take back whatever he said if anyone objected.

I grappled with my high school French. "An angel passes?"

He nodded. "Why am I talking in French? I must be trying to impress you."

My mother laughed a little too loudly. She leaned forward, urging Ellis and me to know and like each other.

"What does it mean?" I asked. My spirits rose with his careful honesty.

"What they say when there's an awkward pause in the conversation."

Both his broad, hammy hands on the wheel, he pulled around double-parked trucks and braked for taxis that cut in front of him as we made our way through the Financial District. So you've been to France?" I asked.

"Me? Oh no. I have a client who listens to tapes in her study while I work." The slight hesitation in his voice seemed to give his listener little places to rest. My mother was smiling.

Another pause, slightly less awkward than the first. "I'm putting in a paneled closet in her master bedroom," he said. "I tried to talk her out of it. It's too lavish for the space, but she says she spends as much time there as any-where else. And wants it nice." He smiled, thought for a couple of beats, and then asked, "So, what's it like to be thirty-four?"

His earnestness, though unnerving, was catching. "Like I'm behind," I said. "Like I woke up one day and all the things I expected to accomplish were suddenly undone."

"What things?"

Mentioning my love life seemed too intense as an opener, so I told him about *Peneaus totecus*. Technically it's a crustacean that's not a real shrimp. It masquerades as a shrimp that cleans parasites off fishes' scales and gills, but instead, *totecus* takes bites from the fishes' very flesh. I was trying to understand how *totecus* managed to gauge how many bites to take to live but not so many as to kill the host.

He nodded, not interrupting with the obviously bored declaration, "I didn't realize prawns were so interest-ing," like my mother's second husband had. With my hip crammed against my mother's, I had the stinging thought that we three could be a family. This was premature, ridic-ulous, but there it was.

The conversation stopped and started in this way until we got to the Embarcadero near the waterfront, and Ellis eased into a parking place that appeared on one of the crowded side streets off Mission. My mother had picked the restaurant—the big square, bricked Boulevard. Its Belle Epoque style suited her; this was one place people might wear hats.

We sat by the large windows facing the street. Ellis got up to make a phone call, and my mother leaned over to me and whispered, "He's not married, not mixed up in some peculiar religion, not even a vegetarian. He may be a lit-tle too busy with work, but you think he's great, I can tell." She looked a little pale, strain showing in the tension of her jaw. She pressed the wells under her eyes with her fin-gertips. I'd underestimated her wish for my approval.

"He's a prince," I said. Too good to be true. My dislike of my mother's lovers had sustained me somehow. I always knew who I was, the logical voice raised against her will-ingness to suspend disbelief. Each man in her life was the kindest, funniest, most responsible man she ever met, that is, until he strayed back to his ex at weak moments or came back from the race track one day with nothing.

Ellis sat down and looked at my mother, then almost wistfully patted her hand on the table. I was becoming a believer.

"I didn't even know this place existed," he said.

My mother smiled. "Stick with me, babe, and I'll show you the world." Her bravado had a tinge of uncertainty or something, I couldn't tell what. The green of her long, shimmering sweater cast a feverish tint on her face.

Ellis laughed. He picked up the wine list and studied

it as hard as he'd studied the traffic, a shy person's ruse. I was utterly charmed.

Mother looked at me, not him, and said, "I took two Imitrex before I got in the truck, but I'm losing the battle here."

So that was it, a headache. She said that her migraines started with a warning aura at the periphery of her vision, then an ache in her right arm, as if it were just waking up from tingly sleep. If she took her medicine and immediately got into bed in complete darkness, she could sometimes head off the worst of it.

She stood and said she would take a cab home before she started throwing up, and that she would be fine, just fine as long as I didn't let this destroy my birthday. With her coat over her arm, she bestowed a kiss on Ellis's forehead, then mine, and was out the door before he or I could say anything.

We looked at each other. "So," he said.

"Here we are," I smiled. My mother often made dramatic entrances and exits, and I had a momentary thought that this was one of those, the headache her unconscious way of intensifying the meeting between Ellis and me. Later, she would breathlessly ask what we talked about and especially what Ellis said about her.

The waiter came and took our order. Ellis ate medallions of beef in Pernot sauce and I had turbot with lime butter. I had often dreamed of eating dinner with a dignified father, the quiet talk, the easy smiles. The fish flaked in my mouth. I ate like a hungry sailor.

My mother's second husband had been a developer of shopping centers. He had a booming voice that embarrassed me in restaurants when he shouted his opinions about the trade deficit and the national debt. One of her lovers told me all about the outrageous alimony he had to pay to two wives, and another explained in detail the ailments he'd had since he was twenty. My mother's exquisite choice of hats seemed matched in some anti-universe by her ruinous taste in men.

The silence lengthened between Ellis and me. I almost got used to it. We finished the bottle of wine. Ellis chewed thoughtfully, smiled at me, looked past the lights twinkling around the windows to a crowd of bicyclists gathering on the misty street corner. The silence tugged at my heart, trying to pull out a long-forgotten memory or feeling. As we ate, our tableware clinking, nostalgia rose through me, an ache for something I'd never known, like a blind person's yearning for color.

I said, "OK. Let's get down to brass tacks. What are your prospects? How is your business doing? Any addictions? Perversions? Vices? I'm not saying they would be deal breakers, but I'd just like to know what they are." I smiled. "After all, this is my mother."

He looked at me with round, blue eyes, the frank gaze, I thought, of a father. "I think," he said, "we need another bottle of pinot." He signaled the waiter and we sat in silence as the steward came and opened the bottle. "I'm thinking," Ellis said as we lifted our glasses, "about moving to Santa Fe next month." He glanced at me and then away.

I felt instantly drunk, as if the wine had suddenly crossed some brain/blood barrier. "My mother can't leave her shop. You know that."

He smoothed his tie. The figures were anchors. "I do know that."

My ears pounded. "You mean—"

"—I don't love your mother."

A frightening number of bicyclists crowded the street. Cars honked at them. "You *can't* mean that." I realized, in that instant, that the bicyclists were the remnants of Critical Mass, riders I sympathized with who took over San Francisco once a month at rush hour, stopping car traffic and insisting on their right to the streets. "You're dumping her?" I asked.

He didn't say anything. Then he slugged back half a glass of wine. "I need to get out of the city. I already have four assistants and if I stay here, I'll need to hire two more." Now he talked fast. "I'm already spending half my time managing the staff and doing bill work. It's driving me crazy."

No. No. No. "You're changing the subject." My voice was too loud. "We're talking about you leaving my mother. You think being fat and bald will get you someone better?" I couldn't believe I said that. A lifetime of feminism out the window.

He rubbed the top of his head. "I didn't want to hurt your mother. I've been trying to get myself to tell her all week, but instead I've been avoiding her."

"Oh, I get it. You know I'll tell her. You saw the opportunity to let me hurt her instead. You coward," I spat. "You want *me* to break my mother's heart."

Suddenly the thought I'd been trying to have all day appeared as clearly as the moon that rose like a balloon above the jostling, laughing, sweaty exuberance of Critical Mass. The bicyclists must have been meeting for a late-evening ride.

"I need you to love my mother," I said softly.

He smiled, pushed down at the corners of his mouth with thumb and forefinger. "She's scared of being ordinary.

I like ordinary. She never gets mad. I don't trust people who are too even-tempered."

"But at first you liked her sense of ceremony," I guessed. "She made you feel like the most extraordinary man in San Francisco. You were walking on air." I felt like I was working out some equation for myself. "And then, when she turned around and loved you, you suddenly weren't so sure."

He pushed at his mouth again, as if smoothing down a goatee. "Maybe," he said.

"Think about it," I cried. "As soon as you knew you could have her, you decided to pick up and leave." I felt hysterical.

He put his hands on the tablecloth. "Your mother tells me you come to San Francisco whenever things heat up in San Diego."

I couldn't deny it.

He said, "We're two peas in a pod. We're the cynics, the spoilers, the rejecters."

"How do you know that about me?"

"Your mother talks about you. She says you've been through a lot of men. She worries about you." I'd never before imagined that my mother had a critical concept of me, the same as I had of her.

Shaken, I said, "I think you're scared. Not that she won't ever touch down to earth, but that she will, and she'll blow your heart apart." I knew it was futile to try to talk him into loving my mother, but I tried anyway.

He reached over and idly folded my mother's napkin. "Do you want to know what I think?"

"No." I was a child.

Silence. "OK. Yes."

"I think you want your mother safely stowed in her

dream before you make a move for yourself. It's the natural order of things. Mother's first. Then daughters."

"Stop. You don't have a right to any armchair whatever."

"Fair enough." A long silence. We both stared at the dwindling crowd of bicyclists.

I drank the last of my water. "I guess dessert is out."

He gave a little laugh. Took a breath. "Let me try again." A pause. "You've probably guessed that my wife died. Shattered me. Age-old story."

I hadn't gotten that far, but of course he had a dead wife. "Was she young?" I asked.

He nodded, holding his mouth steady against seasoned grief. "We were married five years. We lived in San Rafael. I had a studio, this idea that wood was the best medium for sculpture. It darkens at its own pace. As you chisel into it, you never know what you'll find, an immature knot, or just a change in grain. It's like entering someone's body. My pieces were beginning to sell. She took two years to die. Cancer. I took care of her. When I got back to the studio, I had nothing left to give. I could only work for other people, clients." He finished his glass of wine and poured another. "In Santa Fe, I want to try to work on my own again. To face the naked wood, so to speak." He gave a little, slightly self-deprecating laugh.

I thought of my mother sleeping in her apartment, unaware of her fate. I said faintly, "You could try again."

He smiled.

I thought of Douglas sleeping in his apartment. The hysterical tremor passed through me again. A vacancy opened up in me. Scared, I patted Ellis's hand, the way he had patted my mother's. I told him all about Douglas, a random, irrational description zooming from his award last year from the National Academy of Arts and Sciences to the pecan pies he baked some Sundays.

Ellis listened. "You make a good case for him."

I looked up. He cocked his head.

"He's a good guy."

Silence descended on us again.

Shattered, he'd said. Like a supernova. Sending shock waves through the universe.

The last of the bicyclists lifted their feet and rode off into the night. I was bereft, exhausted, out of ideas.

My dead father once brought me a cube of resin preserving a specimen of the elegant Lysmata shrimp, its white antennae splayed out in frozen anticipation of detecting a moving object. This was my first shrimp. I still have the cube. Someday I'm going to Bali to see Lysmata in action, cleaning cardinalfish. I've always thought of going alone. But wasn't Bali Hai a place for two?

"I think," I said, "that we should find me a hat for my birthday."

"I wanted to love your mother," he said softly.

"What is, is." Hadn't that always been my motto?

Possibly because of the early sweep of bicyclists and traffic jams, the city streets seemed deserted, tall office buildings mostly dark. Didn't anyone work late anymore? At night, even the most colorful shrimp turn dark blue, almost impossible for their predators to see. Then the shrimp are free to scavenge.

I had a key to my mother's shop. I snapped on the lights. As usual, I imagined people under the crowd of hats. My father. Ellis's wife. Ones who left too soon. Those who didn't have a fight to call their own, but were missing in action anyway. Intense sadness overtook me. Maybe what I wanted to retrieve from the past didn't exist—a wholeness, a steadfastness between people that I could count on, a faithfulness in my own heart that I'd never been able to create. I thought of Douglas, his perplexed hurt when I came home late without explanation, even though I could easily have called from the lab. I was careless with him, though I condemned carelessness.

Ellis and I tried at least ten hats on me. He lifted each one from its perch and lowered it on my head.

"The problem is, I have my father's Marlboro man face, my mother's build. Not congruent."

"Only stunning."

"Are you flirting with me?"

He looked startled. "No."

"It's OK," I said. "You can flirt with me."

I could see him in the mirror behind my mother's desk. A little smile came to his eyes. "It's hard enough to turn down one of you."

He told me to take out the clip from my hair. I stood in front of the mirrors and together we fluffed out the strands. Unlike my mother, I looked better with my hair around my face; it softened my angular cheekbones. Yet the hats seemed either too big, overwhelming my eyes and making my long face even longer than it was; or too small, perching on my head like little growths. The fashion this year featured hats with very wide brims in heavy materials. I tried on a soft fur by Eugenia Kim and looked like I was being smothered by a large bat. Ellis thought the simple crown of a fedora in straw would suit me, but we agreed that the hat seemed to cut my face in half and emphasize my ears, which are not petite. A Greta Garbo came close to looking good, a dark brown leather hat by Lola came even closer. But in the end, we agreed that I was a lost cause.

It was a joke, but my sadness deepened. Ellis slid off my mother's desk, and we went into the rainy night to see my mother.

I quietly let us in to her darkened place. Tall chairs were black shadows in the dining area. The drawn shades faintly brightened and then went gray with passing car lights. Ellis moved to the kitchen and turned on the single stove light so we could see. Apparently he had tended my mother during a headache before.

She was asleep on her back on the red couch with a velour blanket pulled over her face. She could have been a corpse composed for burial. I thought that someday she might die, without love. The thought was unbearable. For a moment, I stood by her covered feet and couldn't move. Ellis leaned his elbows on the kitchen counter. He seemed willing to let the grief sink around us.

I touched my mother's knee through the blanket. It was muffled bone, its real shape somehow unknowable. She made each moment an event that she never fully entered. She might never change. I needed to wake her, needed to cast off this sense of doom, of something ending. I carefully lifted the blanket from her face and kissed her soft cheek. She smelled of sleep, like a small child. She opened her eyes. "Oh," she said without flinching at my face so close to hers.

"We're here. I just wanted you to know." I didn't move back.

She was so pale that blue shadows fell from her nose and curled at the corners of her mouth. Her skin looked damp, the creases of her eyelids slick. Maybe she'd sensed Ellis's rejection but hadn't yet let the thought reach her consciousness.

She pushed up against the leather pillows. "I'm better," she said.

She knew what I wanted to hear.

"I got you a present," she said. Her voice was hoarse, as if she'd been shouting, though I knew that her headaches kept her very quiet. "Don't turn on the light. You can see it over there on the sideboard."

By the dining area. I moved through the shadows to get a smallish hat box. I didn't want a hat. I'd tried hard enough. Ellis lifted his eyebrows at me. I brought the round box back to my mother.

I knelt on the carpet by my mother's head and opened the blue-striped wrapping paper. A baseball cap with no logo, stone-washed gray green. She must have had it made. Such a concrete, no-nonsense, somehow indisputable object. I put it on, pushed down the back.

"Perfect," Ellis said.

"Yes." Without looking, I could tell it was perfect. Casual. Darkening the area just above my eyes like a small curtain. I kissed my mother again. I smoothed her cheek the way she'd smoothed mine when I was a child. She let me. "I was afraid," she said, "that it was going to take me thirty-*five* years to find you the right one."

"You never give up."

"No," she whispered. "I never give up."

We three sat together. There would be time enough for me to call Douglas and tell him I was staying for a few more days. My assistant had things under control. I got another blanket, Ellis leaned back in his chair, and the moments stretched out in the long quiet I'd just learned to tolerate.

LAKE CRESCENT

I n the motel room Laura stirred. Alex, sitting up beside her, said, "I've been thinking about my brother."

She lifted her head from the pillow. "Actually, I asked about your mother."

He bent and kissed her warm hair, saying nothing.

She smiled. "OK, a brother. Looks like?" She pushed herself up beside him, flank to flank. She had been at the evening reading of his second book on his father. From the audience, she'd asked if he would ever write about his mother.

He'd brushed off the question. His mother was a flash in the night, long gone. He remembered the cool smell of stars. Which stars? Somewhere over the Olympic Peninsula years ago.

In bed at dawn in the Spokane River Falls Motel and Conference Center, Alex felt strange and fragile.

"My brother's name is Jeep," he said. "For Jim. A lawyer in Vancouver. Nice guy." Except when he was drinking, which he hadn't for the last six months. Alex felt a tap, tap of hope, held it back. His brother would do whatever he was going to do.

"I see," she said. "A nice lawyer." She rolled her eyes.

A flicker of pain traveled through him. "I don't need anybody's casual sarcasm right now," he said.

"Whoa." She looked at him.

"Sorry."

A moment passed. "You're supposed to give a little explanation to go with the 'sorry.' Like: 'My brother Jeep is my best fan.'"

"He is my best fan."

She held out her palms.

"Did you know that you're unrelenting?" he asked.

"I've heard that."

Silence again. He felt like crying. No reason. "Tell you what," he said. "I'll go downstairs and get you some coffee from your conference. Doughnuts. We can spend the morning in bed doing nothing. I think we both need a morning off."

"We're *dental* technicians."

He looked at her.

She said. "No doughnuts. Ask the cardiologists. They have the worst habits."

He came back with two coffees and some grapes in a cup. She laughed. She probably should have worn the big hotel robe but she wasn't cold or modest. He might say more if she was in her tank top. They sat on the rumpled covers.

He took a breath. "Actually, this has my mother in it."

"Aha, I wore you down." She pulled a pillow to her lap.

He kissed her and told her about his mother's insomnia and quickly described a few of her small cruelties toward him and his brother, then the strangeness of the day the court called her unfit.

Laura took this in but didn't speak.

Alex continued: "Jeep was a funny guy. He was born funny. If anyone could make her laugh, it was him. Except this one day. It was just a couple of months before Jeep and I moved in with our aunt. One of my mother's catering clients threw herself a huge 50th birthday party. The client's name was Charlize, like the actress. Charlize rented the resort at Lake Crescent."

Laura lifted a brow.

He said, "It's on the Olympic Peninsula."

"I know. Funny place for a party. Middle of a million trees. Nowhere."

"Yes." Alex stopped for a minute, remembering. "That's why Jeep and I were allowed to come. Everyone stayed in the cabins. Charlize's oldest son Beau was twenty, but he took Jeep under his wing and shared his weed with us. For two days he let us hang out with him and his two brothers behind the cabins, even when they got some girls from Port Angeles to show up. For the adults the weekend was a big drunken bash. My mother served ceviche on the pier, flaming steaks in the Roosevelt lodge. Friday and Saturday were freezing—the women wore ski jackets over their dresses—but the party was a big success. Charlize took a shine to my mother and bestowed a nickname on her. Margo. My mother was thrilled. I was ten and took offense—I loved the dignity of Margaret."

"Margaret," Laura said quietly.

He smiled. "Can't get anything past you."

Laura got up, walked to the window and looked out, her bare hip limned by early sun. She bent to the floor and came back with panties in hand.

THE SUN BROKE OUT on Sunday morning. Mountain weather can change in minutes, and by noon the day was hot. Most of the guests had left on the chartered bus, but Charlize's best friends still lounged on big chairs in front of the lodge. Charlize strode out onto the sloping grass lawn and announced that everyone was going swimming across the lake. "Grab your suits and find a boat, everyone!" she said. "Beau, you guys too! Old people and young people together." She turned to her little audience. "I'm old now. I can be a dictator."

Beau shrugged, smiled at his mother.

Margaret started to pick up the iced tea glasses, but Charlize stopped her. "Margo! Come play with us. You deserve a break! You can be in my boat."

"Oh!" Margaret said and flushed. She turned to Alex and said eagerly, "Quick! We don't want to hold anyone up!" In the cabin she frantically threw towels in a soft-sided cooler, which was their newest, least shabby bag. "Hurry, hurry!" she hissed to the boys. Jeep got the shorts he used as a swimsuit and was out the door, racing to join Beau.

"No!" Alex said to his mother. "You go without me." He didn't know why he was against this. His mother loved to swim. That was one thing he knew.

She shook his arm. "You're coming. This is our *chance*."

"For what?"

"I don't know." Red spots lingered on her throat. She looked ready to cry. "She invited us. We're her *guests*." She looked bewildered for a second. "She won't ask again," she said softly, and Alex yanked the bag from her and went to the pier.

Soon, six fishing dinghies manned by the teenagers and some of the resort staff were gliding across the glacier-fed lake. Flicks of icy water hit Alex's face as Beau's brother David rowed a little drunkenly into the hot afternoon.

They gathered at the Devil's Punch Bowl, a small, symmetric bay at the far edge of the immense lake. This bay was spanned by a hump-backed footbridge about fifteen feet above the water. Huge cedars rose even farther up the cliff behind the bridge.

Beau and his brothers slid out of the boats and, hooting from the cold, climbed onto rocks at the side, disappeared into a forest path, and reemerged on the bridge. One by one they climbed over the rail and cannonballed into the lake, trying to swamp the boats while Charlize and the others rowed frantically backward. Charlize screamed happily at her sons, "Wicked! It's ice."

"Your idea, Mom!" Beau yelled from the bridge. "C'mon! What are you waiting for?"

"Don't challenge me!" But she stayed in the boat, laughing. Someone handed her a plastic glass of wine.

Margaret stood up, pulled her sweatshirt over her head, and slid into the water, then quickly pulled herself up on the shelf rock and disappeared onto the path. She appeared on the bridge above. Her suit had bows at the shoulders. She threw her leg over the rail, getting ready to jump.

The other adults looked up from the boats. Alex had heard Charlize say that his mother was cute, as if talking about a puppy. "Go, Margo!" Charlize shouted, raising her glass.

"No!" Alex thought. "No!"

His mother jumped and came up screaming from the cold, like the teenagers. "Wow!" the adults said, leaning out of their boats. Margaret beamed as she held onto the prow of Charlize's boat, her hair streaming over her ears.

Where was Jeep? Alex quietly lowered himself into the water, which was so cold, it burned. He gulped big breaths and handed himself along the boat gunwales to get to the shelf rock and the path. He heard voices above and followed the path past the bridge. The air was a warm benevolence. Up. Up past towering trees. The three brothers were in a little clearing at the top of the cliff, along with Jeep and the girls, who must have come by land somehow. They were standing around making soft jokes, something Alex had never mastered. At school he was a loner, protected by his radar for insult and injury. *The trick was to never get your hopes up. Even when people said you could join their group, you needed to go slow, get ready for them to take it back.* His mother didn't understand that.

He turned to the lake and was astonished at how high they were, about fifty feet, the deep blue water spreading out below, the lodge looking like a building block at the edge, the rainforest beyond. He went away from the group to look again.

Suddenly, Beau dropped the hand of the girl he stood next to, ran straight for the cliff, and jumped! He sailed into the air toward the tiny boats.

His brother David stood up from a log, said, "All right then," sprinted to the edge, and launched himself into thin air! There were screams from below, nightmare screams, then Charlize's delighted voice above the rest, "What am I going to do with you two?! What am I going to do with you?"

Alex, on the other side of the rock, noticed that Jeep stayed in the shadows of the clearing. Jeep was terrified of heights and could barely swim. Alex was surprised he'd somehow made himself jump from the bridge, which now looked tiny and far below.

Beau's other brother—what was his name?—kissed one of the girls, marched to the jumping rock, and sailed through the air.

Alex took a breath. OK, everyone had gotten their moment of glory. No more bodies flying past him. He and Jeep could quietly go down the path. But in minutes Beau and David came up through the forest again, followed by Alex's mother. What was she doing here? Without hesitation, David walked solemnly to the jumping rock, said, "Farewell, sweet world!" and jumped.

"Next!" Margaret said excitedly, stepping up to the rock.

"No!" Alex cried.

His mother barely turned to his voice, then back. The shock of the height rippled through her. Her jaw turned white. She pushed out two panicked breaths. Alex saw what she saw. The vast world of blue and green. For the first time, he realized how small she was. Her suit had a giant bow at the back between her shoulder blades. The smaller bows wavered on her shoulders like butterflies. She looked like a kid.

Below, Charlize's voice bounced up from the water. "Hey, Margo! Wow, Margo! You're going to do it!"

"Gotta hold up the honor of the old folks!" Margaret yelled down, swaying on the rock.

Alex took three quick steps to her and grabbed her arm, but she shook him off and stared down at Charlize with heaving breaths. Without turning, she said to Alex, "Sometimes you just have to take a chance."

"No," Alex said. "They know how to jump. We don't." She looked so strange and pale that he didn't touch her again.

Jeep came up to her, saying quietly, "Mom, Mom. Don't."

Alex thought for a second that she was convinced, but

then Beau called from the sidelines, "Watch out, Jeep! Momma's gonna show you up! Go first! Show her how it's done, my man."

Jeep turned to him. "Not on your life!" He comically held out his hands like an impresario. "Only fools and dogs would jump from here." He must have heard that somewhere.

A chant rose from below, "Go, Jeep, go! Go, Margo, go!"

"Do it!" Margaret said to Jeep. "You know how!" Her eyes were wide, her hands out as she leaned toward her son.

The chant rose. "Go, Margo! Go, Jeep! Go! Go!"

Jeep cried, "Whoa, Mom! Chill." He took her elbow, but she turned to stare at the crowd below, and Alex thought he had never seen anyone so lonely, a tiny figure against the rising afternoon breeze. There was a moment. She stood quietly next to Jeep, unspeaking, and then she turned and pushed him with both hands, and he plunged backward over the cliff, arms wheeling.

He flew through the air upside down, his back to the cliff. He was going to hit the rocks. Alex gasped. His mother put her hands to her mouth and wailed, then stopped in silent horror. What would happen next? The chanting stopped and the silence was a heaviness in the ears as Jeep, in the air, pulled his knees up tight, a slow-motion ball, spinning.

Margaret jumped, a tiny bead of desperate faith in the unknown. And then, as if he'd practiced all his life, Jeep threw out his legs and torqued into a lovely arced dive and knifed into the water about five feet from the closest boat. There was silence. More silence. Margaret plunged in nearby. And then Jeep burst to the surface, screaming, "Whoo-oo!" and then, "Jee-zus! Jee-zus!" And his mother surfaced with a shout, screaming, "You did it! See! You did it!" and Alex sat in the dirt high above and felt a loneliness like blindness blotting out the sun, people, grass, trees, water.

BEFORE THE READING, ALEX thought he'd parked his rented car close to the bookstore, but couldn't find the place. His publicist had said it was underground, look for a wide door on North Elm. He walked through downtown Spokane. No Elm. He was late. He passed a Jehovah's Witness building, crossed at the light. An older woman hunched low in a Camry slowed to let him pass while she turned right. Almost slowed. He walked faster to get around her, but she was blind to him and kept approaching; he yelped high and weird, a frightened animal, as her bumper brushed his jeans. She startled, one hand up, but the car continued on and he panted as he stood at the curb.

OK. He was OK, just exhausted. Two more nights in Spokane and he could go home to his own bed. He was at the end of a long book tour, not in existential peril. His auntie and her husband had raised him and Jeep in a rambling house in Port Orchard, one ferry ride from Seattle. Alex had that house now. His auntie was really his great aunt, not even a very close relative. Alex thought of her and her husband as his parents.

When Alex got home, he would fix himself some scrambled eggs, then walk down the path and into the surf. His evening ritual. He would make himself dive, without hesitation, into the surging iciness of Puget Sound.

BESIDE HIM, LAURA DIDN'T move. Moments passed. The sun caught the windows of a tall building across the street. She took his hand. "You're Jeep's fan, too."

He nodded. For a while, they didn't move.

AFTER THE READING, HE and Laura had discovered they were staying in the same motel and he'd offered her a ride. He left her in the lobby, telling her that jet lag was catching up with him. He needed to stretch out in the foreign room, maybe doze, not think.

He dropped his messenger bag in his room and washed his face. The mirror in the tiny bathroom quickly steamed. He rubbed a circle. Blurry Man with Halo. His fatigue took on a strange edginess. That Camry coming at him. He needed a night cap. He'd seen a bar area in one corner of the lobby with a sign that said something about free wine.

There she was, standing next to a stool with her hand on the stem of a heavy wine glass filled almost to the top. The clerk/bartender handed a bald man a plastic key and came over to Alex. "Can I get you anything?"

"I'll have what she's having."

She pulled a scrunchie out of her hair so it cascaded onto her shoulders. He didn't like it when women fiddled with their hair.

"Are you stalking me?" he asked pleasantly.

She pulled the scrunchie over her index finger and shot it at him.

He laughed. The raw wine felt oddly good in his throat. The day held no crisis, just someone who'd momentarily forgotten how to drive. Plus, it had produced this person, this ... interesting glitch. She'd refreshed the scent that he'd barely noticed in the car, like a memory returned.

"Laura?" he asked. Maybe Monica?

She tilted her head. "Right." A sip. "The one from your commute fifteen minutes ago."

"Fair enough." Fine hands on the polished bar. Short nails. No polish. He added, "Readings make me crazed."

She shrugged. "I was heckling. At the reading. I don't know what got into me."

"How did you know I had a mother?"

The smile created a dimple on one side. "Googled. I read up on people, go to events. My job...not a lot of job satisfaction. I'm in a phase, waiting for something to happen, or someone to tell me how to live. A transition." She looked up. "TMI?"

"Well, *yes.*"

She raised a brow. "You haven't had enough free wine."

Oddly, he imagined her shouting, like he had done. "Are you married?" he asked.

"Somewhat." A pause. "You?"

He shook his head. "But you already knew that."

She laughed.

That easy laugh, her sweet piano hands.

His wife Catherine couldn't get any traction with him; so often, he was someplace else. He tried to think about whatever she was saying—her job at the Koolhaas library downtown, the interesting man on the Bainbridge ferry— but his mind would travel to the article he'd read on coho salmon or the smell of his auntie's soda bread. He loved his wife and didn't want her to leave. He tried to concentrate but one day she was gone, and a few weeks later, she sent a van to pick up half the furniture, and suddenly he had half a stage to act his life. Jeep—who by then had been married three times—encouraged Alex to do something, write something, get his mind off his troubles. That was the start of his first book.

Laura and Alex went upstairs to his room. He sat in the one big chair in the room and she sat on his lap, fully clothed. At first, they didn't speak or move. The rain had stopped. The building across the street was a black rectangle, except for a single light on the fifth floor. That light went out and the one in the office next door came on. She said, "The janitor."

"No, the light from a distant galaxy, just now reaching our eyes."

She shook her head. "Writers." She slid her hand under his shirt. "Even I know a janitor is much better than a star."

"Everyone's a critic."

She laughed and pulled him up. "So watch out."

He awoke in the dark. Someone had turned off the lights. She was still there. Relief hit him so hard he winced. Drapes still open. The light from the building across the street had traveled down to the far right office, ground floor, near the door. The janitor ready to go home to his wife.

Jeep had saved Alex after his divorce. When they were kids, Jeep had saved them both. One October night he pulled Alex out of bed in the yellow house and told him they were leaving. He showed Alex the money he'd taken from their mother's good purse. They'd use it for the bus fare and the ferry to their aunt's place. They'd ask for protected status. He snapped on the light.

Alex held his arm over his eyes. "Protected status is for animals."

Jeep stuffed jeans from the floor in his backpack. "Auntie said we could come any time. Did you take my water bottle?" Their mother slept across the hall.

It was almost dawn. So dark. "We can't leave her. It's not nice."

Jeep hit him with his pack. "You have three minutes."

Alex lay on his back in the motel room. Laura slept

with her cheek resting against the crook of his arm. She'd kissed him there, and his palm, slow, moving with no hurry toward the folds of balls and ass. Maybe he dozed. His mind burrowed further backward and hit a near-memory, an experience lost to him like a file in a computer buried by a bit of broken code. Though hidden from Alex, the experience was intact and alive, radiating sorrow and guilt through all of his life. He was six years old, just before the age of reason, and already accustomed to a blur of nights and days by his mother's sleeping habits. He awoke to noises in her room and went past Jeep snoring lightly in the big bed by the door. She had her bright blue swimsuit on and was laughing with a shirtless man in tuxedo pants. The man sat on the bed. He smelled like mustard, a deep and dangerous vinegar. Jeep had told Alex that their father left when their mother was pregnant with him.

When Alex was very young, he'd woken a few times and gone to her. Then, he'd sensed that someone was in her room but couldn't see anyone. Twice, she angrily scooped him up and dumped him in his bed. "You're supposed to be sleeping," she hissed. "Be a big boy. Go to sleep."

So he knew not to interrupt and instead hid behind the doorjamb and looked through the crack.

"We have to go fast," his mother said to the man. "They sleep like logs until about four. Then anything. Once, I found them eating graham crackers and jelly on the floor in the garage."

The man reached out and gathered her between his legs, but she laughed—high and strange—and pulled away. Alex had heard that laugh before. He went back and climbed through his bedroom window, dropped down beside the bush there and watched at the corner of the house, unseen. He heard rustling, then the man came out on the front walk and she followed, turned, and locked the front door. Alex realized that she thought she was locking him in. But he was out. A sense of wrongness draped over him. The stars sent a chill onto dewy wet leaves that touched his pajamas. He was afraid but not crying. He followed his mother, who walked down the shadowy street, laughing and talking almost nonstop while the man pulled at her and she pulled away. In his mind Alex laughed too. He didn't get the joke, but thought this would help her. She needed help. She was headed to the pond down the road, called Two Ponds.

She stopped in the street.

Alex stopped. He stood in the shadow of a parked car.

"I'm a good mother," she said solemnly to the man.

"The best," the man he said loudly.

She touched the man's arm. "Maybe this isn't a good idea."

Alex patted the car. He could tell he was helping her, but his heart was high and painful.

They walked again. Alex walked. If he did what she did, he would keep her safe, drawing her danger to himself. Then he would hide it away, like the samples he took of his mother's party things, paper drink umbrellas, small Jelly Belly boxes for a rich kid's birthday, real silver dollars. He was good at hiding things. He was confident about this.

At the pond the man took off his pants. He walked straight into the water in his baggy boxers as if it wasn't cold. She followed. When Alex went in, the icy shock surprised him. He crouched behind the end of the waterslide. He couldn't swim yet. His mother was a good swimmer, but she and the man just splashed water at each other like little kids. Alex splashed also, unheard in the melee. A group of teenagers stood at the far edge of the parking lot, smoking, low voices.

Alex waded in deeper, velvet mud at his feet. The stars were holes and the sky was escaping through them. Jeep had explained this. Alex panicked. Jeep said the sky would one day deflate like a huge balloon. Their mother swam toward the dark middle of the pond, and the man came up to her and dunked her. She rose up laughing, gasping, the water spilling off her shoulders. To accompany her, Alex went down but came up quickly to check on her, and the man was holding her under again, her hands waving frantically.

"No!" Alex shouted but they didn't hear. What could he do? Nothing. He went down with her. He didn't want her to be alone under the water. He pushed up. She was up! It worked! She swam fast back toward shore. "No breath!" she shouted. "Too cold!" The man caught up with her.

"You looked like a cartoon!" he said. "So funny!" They sculled in the deep water with just their heads above the surface.

"Not funny," she gasped, coughing. She started to swim away, and he took her shoulders from behind. "Stop!" she screamed. "Not funny!" He shoved her under.

Alex went down. He had to stay down with her. He could tell she wasn't coming up again. She was out of breath. No breath. He wouldn't come up either. His chest went back and forth seeking air. No air, just that huge tug at nothingness. His pajamas were weights. He would stay with her. Stay with her. Stay.

He shot up and gasped. Life flooded back. Without words, he knew he had left her, betrayed her. Water and night sky tumbled together. He was damned. He did not think this; he knew it. A boy does not leave his mother alone with all her dangers. He was shut out of the world.

The teenagers found Alex semiconscious on the end of the plastic slide and called 911. The cops brought him home. His mother answered the door in her robe and screamed when she saw him wearing a huge gray hoodie and clinging to a policewoman. His mother had come back home without investigating the cause of the sirens, then had sent the man packing and stepped into the shower. To the police, she didn't mention her trip to the pond. She said she had no idea why her son had climbed out his bedroom window and gone swimming in the middle of the night.

"I have a six-year-old," the policewoman said gently. "They're capable of anything."

THE BOOKSTORE AUDIENCE HAD been surprisingly large—maybe thirty people—some of them finishing ice cream in small cups. Alex had read a passage from his new book on his father's work, describing the first time he saw his father's massive stone couch installed at the Portland airport. The Oregon rain had pounded on the airport roof, amplifying the jarring sense of his father's art, a domestic object made huge and looming.

Alex explained that his book was a journey into his father's body of work. A critic's memoir of viewing each massive installation for the first time. Mostly, he left out the man, his imperious, drunken father, the late sculptor James Haugen whom Alex met three times. Haugen had driven away agents, assistants, siblings, and wives; children, he simply left.

Alex read well, but in his mind, he heard his gruff, animal yelp as the Camry grazed him. That sound jarred something loose. A woman at the front nodded. The frightened shout rose in his thoughts again. He'd heard that sleep deprivation was more effective than out-and-out torture to break a captured spy.

A balding man said in a tremulous voice that he'd made and loved the lemon-tarragon chicken from Alex's first book, called *An Artist's Would-Be Cookbook*, which was a compilation of recipes his father Haugen had scribbled on napkins, Post-it Notes, sketches and unpaid bills. Alex thanked the man for his kind words.

The woman at the front stood up. Usually people raised their hands or just dove in with questions. Beside her, a brick wall permanently oozed mortar. About his age. Heels. Denim.

"Laura," she said, as if everyone would want to know her. "Book one," she said, "Your father's recipes." She pushed at her hair. "Book two—your father's art. Book three. Your mother?"

He rarely thought about her anymore. She'd moved to Sydney, started her catering company again, and died at forty-three of an aneurysm. She was long gone, but an image shot into his mind of her small yellow house. He ran his hand down the front of his shirt.

His mother stood beside the house with arms crossed, her raincoat swirling. She was small and erect, a caterer who could calm a bride, then go back to the trucks and fire two drivers for showing up late. She was an insomniac. When the boys were very young, she'd pull them out of bed in the middle of the night, give them cups of grainy cocoa, and make them cuddle with her while she watched reruns. As they got older, she commanded them to rewash all the dishes, weed by flashlight. Her rages grew like the morning glory strangling the downspout in the side yard.

Alex closed the book in front of him and said steadily, "We can't write about our mothers. They can't be known. They blaze. All of them. Even the quiet ones. Our hearts get confused when we think about them. They're monoliths. Too huge for words." He smiled. He'd seen videos of himself doing OK at a podium even while his mind raced.

The woman wasn't deterred. "Other people write about their mothers."

"That they do." He smoothed the cover of the book. "Looks like I need to catch up on my Sherman Alexie."

She frowned, pushed at her messy ponytail.

"Let me put that on hold," he said. A small peace offering.

Others in the audience asked good questions about his writing, which they called process. Two bought books.

As he was climbing the stairs to street level, the one who had asked about his mother caught up with him. He opened the heavy door onto huge raindrops falling through the street lights. She produced an umbrella and they discovered they were in the same motel. He offered her a ride. They walked the streets toward his car. There was the exciting smell of water on asphalt.

He took over holding the umbrella. She glanced up at him and smiled.

"My mother tried so hard to teach me how to swim," he said. Nothing more.

Her smile faded, then quickly returned. "I see." She took his arm. "End of story," she teased.

There was the sound of splashing everywhere.

ACKNOWLEDGMENTS

Many of these stories have been previously published:

"One Small Death Before the Plague" in *Free State Review*

"Atlantis" in *Eureka Literary Magazine* (with the title "Revocable Family Trust")

"Slide It Closer to the Center" in *Sou'wester* (with the title "Move It Closer to the Center")

"Wild Oats" in *Arts and Letters* (with the title "Self-Made Man")

"Hawk Wind" in the *North American Review* (with the title "Trapper Lake")

"A Place for Fine Hats" in *TriQuarterly*

"Lake Crescent" in *Louisville Review* (with the title "Forty-Two Degrees")

"Listen" *New Ohio Review*

Pamela Gullard's recent work has appeared in *Arts & Letters*, *The North American Review*, *Free State Review*, *TriQuarterly* and *Sou'wester*. She has won a PEN Syndicated Fiction Project Award and the H.G. Roberts Fiction Writing Award judged by Gordon Lish. *Breathe at Every Other Stroke*, her previous collection, includes stories that appeared in *The Iowa Review* and others. She teaches literature at Menlo College and lives with her husband Mike in nearby Menlo Park, California. They have two sons who also love to read.